HUNGRY FOR LOVE

When celebrity chef Charlie Irons is let go from his daytime cookery slot, Louise Drew becomes his replacement. But with minimal cookery experience, appalling on-air nerves and disastrous culinary experiments, she is unable to sustain viewing figures and is sacked. She applies for a new job as a personal assistant with catering experience, but realises to her horror that it would mean working for Charlie Irons — and looking after two headstrong young girls. Is Louise up to the task, especially when Charlie's glamorous ex-wife arrives on the scene?

MARGARET MOUNSDON

HUNGRY
FOR LOVE

Complete and Unabridged

LINFORD
Leicester

First published in Great Britain in 2017

First Linford Edition
published 2017

A catalogue record for this book is available
from the British Library.

ISBN 978–1–4448–3509–0

Published by
F. A. Thorpe (Publishing)
Anstey, Leicestershire

Set by Words & Graphics Ltd.
Anstey, Leicestershire
Printed and bound in Great Britain by
T. J. International Ltd., Padstow, Cornwall

This book is printed on acid-free paper

1

Louise stared in disbelief at the man sitting behind the desk. He raised an eyebrow. 'Lost for words, Ms Drew?' he taunted.

She swayed, clutched the edge of the desk and managed to gasp, 'You,' before her throat muscles contracted.

'Me, indeed,' he agreed with a sardonic smile.

Louise closed her eyes. *Personal assistant with catering experience needed, accommodation provided.* She recited the advert in her head. She should have known it was too good to be true.

She opened her eyes. It wasn't a bad dream. He was still there.

'I'm sure I must be the last person in the world you want to see right now,' he voiced her feelings with one-hundred-percent accuracy.

Louise made a faint noise of

acknowledgement at the back of her throat before annoyance kicked in. 'I don't enjoy having my time wasted,' she snapped.

'Neither do I.'

'Well, now that you've had your fun, if you'll excuse me . . . ' She swung the strap of her bag over her shoulder. 'I have to find a job.'

'Not so fast,' he stalled. 'I haven't finished with you yet.'

'Maybe not, but I've finished with you.'

'What went wrong?' His soft question wrong-footed her.

'What do you mean?'

'Exactly what I say.'

'You know what went wrong,' she scoffed.

'Actually, I don't.'

'I was let go.' Louise tossed back her head. 'There, are we finished now?'

'It hurts, doesn't it, to know you're no longer wanted.'

A flush of shame worked its way up Louise's neck.

'I was told a younger, fresher image was needed,' he continued. 'What happened to you?'

'Viewing figures plummeted after I took over.' Louise's voice was so low that Charlie had to lean forward to hear what she was saying. 'They pulled the programme.'

'That's a shame. It was a good format.'

Six months earlier, after celebrity chef Charlie Irons had been outsourced, Louise Drew had been promoted from back-room girl to take his place. The decision had been met with universal outrage. With minimal cookery experience, appalling on-air nerves and disastrous culinary experiments, she had been unable to sustain viewing figures. Charlie's loyal fan base deserted the programme in droves. Louise limped on for a few desperate weeks before she had been called into the production office on a dismal Monday morning. As rain battered the huge glass windows, she was given the bad news. Not only had she lost the cookery slot, but her services were no longer

3

required at the station.

No one likes a loser had been one of her colleague's parting shots. Louise had subsequently been dubbed 'Louise the Loser' by sections of the media, and the name had stuck. Carrying her personal possessions in a black bin liner and feeling like a criminal, her fall from grace had been complete when a member of security had escorted her off the premises. She knew her rapid promotion had been resented by some of her more experienced colleagues and that they weren't sorry to see her go. No one said goodbye and no one waved to her from the windows of the glass-plated building she had called home for the past two years.

Hashtags sprang up on media platforms overnight. Everyone, it seemed, had views on her dismissal, most of which were uncomplimentary. There was even a movement to get Charlie Irons reinstated. When he wasn't cooking, he had entertained viewers with stories of his childhood and his adored fisherman grandfather who had been responsible for bringing him up. Grandpa Irons had been part of the package, and the audience loved hearing about him as much as they loved listening to Charlie.

Louise frowned at the dishevelled man sitting behind the desk opposite her. At the moment he didn't look much like a celebrity chef. He had the appearance of someone who hadn't slept for a week.

At the time of his dismissal there had been rumours of personal problems, but no one knew for sure if they were true. Charlie was notoriously reclusive about his private life, even going so far as to insist that those working around him sign a privacy clause.

He was now doing his best to stifle a yawn. 'Sorry.' He flapped an apologetic hand at her.

Louise refused to indulge in any sympathy. 'If you're seeking revenge, then congratulations — I fell for your story hook, line and sinker. I really thought there was a job on offer.'

'There is.' Charlie's eyes now watered

as he stifled a second yawn.

'You got me here under false pretences.' She leaned forward and, placing both hands on the desk, looked him straight in the eye. He backed off in alarm. 'To save you the trouble of gloating any further, let me update you on my situation. I'm currently unemployed and desperate for work. I've sold my car to pay the rent. Unless I find somewhere to live within the next few days, I'll be out on the streets.' She held up a hand as he tried to interrupt, her turquoise eyes as cold as a winter sea. 'Since being dismissed from a job I loved, I've learned not to trust anyone. I've also developed the skin of a rhinoceros, so feel free to say your piece now.' She stepped back and, feeling like Joan of Arc as she prepared to face the flames, finished with, 'Cruel words no longer have the power to hurt me.'

'That's good.' Charlie's lopsided smile had been a hit with his viewers, especially ladies of a certain age, but right now its effect was lost on Louise.

She was fighting to retain the last vestiges of her dignity. 'A rhinoceros hide is exactly what I'm looking for.'

He towered over Louise as he stood up. Her eyes now clashed with the middle button of his crumpled shirt. She noticed that several of the other buttons were missing.

'You've had your say,' he insisted. 'Now it's my turn. Please — ' He indicated the chair. ' — won't you sit down again?'

'I prefer to stand.'

'That's as may be, but I've been up all night and I'd like to sit down, and my grandfather always taught me it was rude for a gentleman to sit in the presence of a lady, so if you wouldn't mind . . . ?'

Louise stood her ground. 'I don't believe you've ever referred to me as a lady before, and I've never thought of you as a gentleman.'

'Look, are you going to sit down or not?' Charlie asked in a testy voice. 'My feet are killing me.'

With a reluctant shuffle, Louise obliged. She wouldn't like to guess what he had been doing all night. One of the unofficial on-set rumours suggested he had been dropped due to his social life affecting his punctuality and professionalism.

'Thank you. Now, where were we?'

'Rhinoceros skins?' An involuntary smile curved the corner of her generous mouth.

'What's so funny?' Charlie demanded.

'You are.'

'I beg your pardon?'

'If your devoted fans could see you now, they'd be in for quite a shock.'

Charlie opened his mouth as if to protest, then rubbed a hand over his designer stubble with a rueful smile and straightened up in his seat. 'To get back to the business of the day, are you interested in taking on the job?'

'You mean there really is one?' Louise's voice went up an octave.

Charlie winced. 'Keep it down. I've had a long night.'

'Have you just offered me the

position of personal assistant?'

'We can discuss job titles later, but I rather believe I have.'

'I'll take it.'

A fleeting look of relief briefly crossed Charlie's tired face. 'Before we discuss details or benefits, there's something I feel I should tell you.'

Louise sagged. Of course there would be a snag. There always was.

'You say here,' Charlie continued, glancing down at her email, 'that you're adaptable?'

'I'll do anything, so long as it's legal.'

'I have an eight-year-old daughter.' He raised his eyes towards Louise.

'I didn't know you were married.'

'I'm not anymore.'

'I see.'

'Fern is part of the deal.'

'The deal?'

'I can't always be around to look after her. I need help.'

'What sort of help?'

'Day to day?' Charlie asked hopefully.

'What about her mother?'

9

'Pia travels a lot. Obviously she helps out whenever she can, but not on a regular basis. That's why Fern lives with me.'

'Wouldn't a trained nanny be better suited to look after your daughter? My experience of eight-year-old girls isn't extensive. Actually, it's nonexistent.'

'Nannies don't seem to stay.' Charlie wriggled uncomfortably in his chair.

'Why not?'

'Differences of opinion,' he mumbled.

'You'll have to give me more than that.'

'Things can get a bit fraught on occasion.'

His reply convinced Louise her suspicions were correct. 'I'm your last hope, aren't I?'

'I wouldn't put it quite like that.'

'I would. You can't get anyone else to stay, can you?'

'It hasn't been easy finding the right person, I'll admit.'

'And you don't get fraught on occasions; you get impossible.'

'Now hold on a moment — '

'I've seen research assistants reduced to quivering wrecks after you've laid into them,' Louise stated. 'I've found colleagues weeping in corridors because they've forgotten to put the right mineral water in your dressing room. And don't get me started on the poor make-up girls.'

'There's no need to go on,' Charlie responded in an arctic voice.

Louise ignored him. 'Everyone had to tiptoe around your monster ego, and then we had to pretend you were Mr Nice Guy when we were interviewed.'

'You don't understand how stressful it can be presenting a daily television slot.'

'Actually, I do.'

They were both breathing heavily as they squared up to each other across the desk.

'Look, do you still want the job or not?' Charlie demanded.

'Anything else you haven't told me about?'

'I have a teenage niece who lives with us on and off.'

'In that case I want raised benefits — two rates of pay if I'm going to act as nanny and personal assistant.'

Charlie looked ready to explode, and Louise began to fear she had gone too far. She was also beginning to feel light-headed, a condition she put down to her lack of breakfast.

Charlie was the first to crack. He passed a weary hand over his eyes. 'You may not know this, but it's half term.'

'I must admit that fact had escaped me.'

'I spent all day yesterday with my daughter at an adventure park. We went on every ride and participated in all the extra activities she could find until I ran out of cash. Then I worked through the night. Fern was up and ready for action again at half past six.'

'Where's your daughter now?' Louise asked.

As if in answer to her question, the door crashed back against the wall and a blonde-haired dynamo raced into the room. She ground to a halt in front of Louise. 'Who are you?' She looked her up and down.

'My name is Louise Drew.'

'What are you doing here?'

'Ms Drew is going to be my new assistant,' Charlie explained. 'Introduce yourself nicely, Fern.'

'I don't like her.' Fern crossed her arms in an aggressive stance, the expression on her face bearing an uncanny resemblance to that of her father's.

'Right now,' Louise confided before Charlie could reprimand his daughter, 'I don't much like you either.'

The look of outrage on Fern's face had Charlie bursting into laughter. Unable to stop herself, Louise joined in.

'You're both silly — and old,' was Fern's parting shot as she stomped out of the office.

After a brief pause, Charlie asked hopefully, 'Do you still want the job?'

Louise hesitated.

'You can have your two rates of pay,' he coaxed.

'Any other shocks you haven't told me about?'

'I can't think of any. Do we have a deal?'

Louise made up her mind. 'We do,' she said, nodding.

'In that case — ' Charlie extended his hand. ' — welcome to the Dover Sole.'

2

Over the next week, Louise began to suspect she might have made a serious error of judgement. Charlie could be charming, stubborn, difficult, magnetic and infuriating — all in the space of five minutes.

'What is a *ferme auberge*?' Louise demanded after he had terminated yet another fruitless telephone call.

The first lesson she had learned when dealing with Charlie Irons was not to bother with being polite, or to consider his finer feelings. If she had, she would not have survived past day one. Charlie was used to the volatile atmosphere of a thriving catering establishment where high tempers were a part of everyday life. Louise realised she was going to have to learn to adjust if she wanted to survive the experience.

They were seated in the upper storey

of what had once been a working out-house. Below them was a roomy vacant barn that Charlie was planning to develop into his new restaurant. Across the courtyard was a surprisingly comfortable farmhouse where he lived. Louise had been given her own large room with sweeping views of the Sussex Downs. For all his faults, Charlie was not mean. Her room had been decorated to the highest standard. The shower cubicle was stocked with an impressive range of expensive toiletries, and to greet her on arrival a sponge in the shape of a yellow duck had been placed on the window-sill. 'A present from Fern,' he explained when Louise tried to thank him.

Fern peered round from behind her father's legs and, scowling, poked her tongue out at Louise. Louise longed to return the gesture but felt the dignified reaction would be to thank the child politely. Her gratitude was met with an indifferent shrug before Fern scuffed out of the room.

The first few days proved more than

difficult, with everyone adjusting to the new domestic arrangements. But now with Fern on a sleepover at a friend's house, this was Louise and Charlie's first chance to talk about his plans for the future.

'A *ferme auberge* is a sort of gastro establishment attached to a farm. You see them a lot in France. They provide good fresh produce, and as well as being restaurants they're social hubs. People come to gossip, enjoy a glass of wine and have a meal. We could perhaps develop a garden area for families to enjoy, things like that.'

'There's no working farm near here providing fresh produce,' Louise pointed out.

Charlie cast her an impatient look. 'I intend where possible to limit food miles and only use locally sourced ingredients.'

'How far away is the nearest farm?' Louise persisted.

'I'm not too sure.'

'Then shouldn't you find out?'

'We don't have to have a farm on our

doorstep.' The stubborn look was back on Charlie's face.

'I thought you said — '

'A source of reliable suppliers of the highest quality is what I need,' Charlie snapped back, 'and I'm not having much luck.'

'I'd noticed,' Louise replied, wondering if she had the nerve to point out that if he exercised a little more patience and tempered his approach, he might get a better reaction from potential suppliers.

'If things carry on like this, we'll be seriously behind schedule,' he said.

'Do you have a time frame in mind?'

Charlie ran a hand through his unkempt hair. He was dressed in his usual checked shirt and baggy jeans, a striking contrast to the chef's whites he had always worn when presenting his cookery slot. 'Two months?' He looked hopefully at Louise.

She greeted his answer with a hollow laugh. 'Two years, more likely.'

'What makes you such an expert on

setting up a restaurant?' he flared up.

Louise bit her lip, fearing they might be in for another of their frank exchanges of views. 'I'm not an expert on anything,' she was forced to admit.

'Tell me something new.'

Louise ignored the jibe. 'But I do know if you think you can convert an abandoned barn into an upmarket restaurant in the space of two months, then you've got more than a challenge on your hands.'

'Right,' Charlie said with a nod, never one to hold a grudge, 'then let's get cracking.'

'What exactly do you want me to do, apart from helping to look after Fern?'

Charlie's daughter had been another area of challenge. She was the apple of her father's eye, and never lost an opportunity to manipulate her position to Louise's disadvantage. Charlie would not hear a word against her, and if Louise hadn't been so desperate for a job, she would have seriously considered resigning.

Charlie always worked late into the night, and his meticulous plans had taken hours of preparation. Louise had been detailed to transpose them onto a spreadsheet. 'They're all in order,' he'd said as he left them on Louise's desk. 'Take care not to muddle them up.'

It was Fern who discovered the sheets of paper scattered all over the floor. The child had been standing suspiciously close to the open window and had immediately gone to find her father to break the news.

Reluctant to blame a possibly innocent child, Louise had accepted full responsibility for the incident and, after receiving a humiliating tongue-lashing from Charlie, had spent over an hour putting the plans back into the right order. After that she made sure that whenever she left the office, the door was locked and the key placed safely in her pocket.

Her bedroom also became a no-go area after Louise discovered the contents of her make-up bag strewn across her dressing table and the door to her fitted wardrobe swinging ajar, her clothes disturbed.

Charlie was now busy inspecting his paperwork. 'If you're looking for a job description,' he said in reply to her query, 'there isn't one. The only thing I insist on is no talking to the media.'

'Why should the media be interested in us?'

'Not us. Me.'

The ringing of his mobile interrupted them. He inspected the caller display. 'I need to take this one,' he said.

He strode out of the office, leaving Louise facing a perplexing list of costs and estimates. The architect's plans stipulated precise requirements to adhere to in order to comply with the stringent building regulations attached to a project of this magnitude, all of which had to be inspected and double-checked by council officials. The slightest infringement, Charlie had informed her, could set them back days. More than once his plans had fallen foul of an overzealous inspector and work had to be redone. How anyone was expected to understand the maze of officialdom was beyond Louise; and with his chef's volatile temperament, she was surprised Charlie hadn't decided that running his own restaurant was all too much bother.

He strode back into the office to the accompaniment of cheerful hammering above a blaring radio. 'That was Quentin Voisin,' he said.

'Isn't he the food critic who writes for the Sunday supplements?'

'One bad review from him and you might as well close down overnight.'

'What does he want with us? I mean, you're hardly in a position to offer him your signature *tarte tatin*.'

'It seems he and Pia, my ex-wife, were doing a promotion together, and she mentioned my plans for the Dover Sole. He expressed an interest in the project.'

'And?' Louise asked, still mystified as to the exact reason for the critic's call.

'He's in the area on Friday and

would like to drop by to see how things are going.'

'What are you going to show him?'

'I thought maybe I could kill two birds with one stone. I could offer him a quick guided tour of what we've done so far, then a basic meal — something along the lines of a really good battered cod with fresh new potatoes and spring vegetables, followed by . . . ' He quirked a smile at Louise. ' . . . apple tart?'

'Does he eat that sort of thing? I mean, wouldn't his first choice of fish be smoked salmon and Dover sole?'

'Possibly, but I intend to do things differently.'

'What if he doesn't like it?'

'He can't close us down if we haven't opened yet, can he?'

'I suppose not.'

'Good, that's settled then. Friday is three days away, so that gives us plenty of time to tidy up. I'll have a word with the builder's foreman and ask him to lay off doing anything noisy while Quentin's here.'

'What's he like?' Louise asked.

'I've never met him,' Charlie admitted, 'but it's best to be prepared. See if you can get Mrs Tolley to dig out a decent tablecloth and matching cutlery.' He grabbed up his keys.

'Where are you going?'

'To source some fresh cod.'

'Good luck,' Louise called after him, then wondered what on earth was she thinking. Charlie Irons made his own luck. Apart from his unfortunate dismissal from the television studio, he always landed on his feet, although she couldn't help wondering why he had such an aversion to personal publicity. She had read several of his interviews, but she felt none of them scratched the surface of the real man underneath.

She settled down and made some notes about what would be needed for Quentin's impending visit, then hurried back to the farmhouse in search of Mrs Tolley.

'There you are,' the homely housekeeper greeted her with a beaming smile.

'I was about to come looking for you.'

'If you want Mr Irons, I'm afraid he's gone out.'

'No matter. I'll pass the message on to you. I've had Miss McDonald on the telephone.'

'Miss McDonald?' Louise looked blank.

'Mrs Irons that was,' Mrs Tolley explained. 'She uses her maiden name professionally. She's Pia McDonald.'

Louise gaped at her. 'The model?'

'That's right. Did you see her photo on the cover of that society magazine last week?' Mrs Tolley was still smiling. 'There's a copy about the place somewhere.' She pulled a glossy magazine out of the newspaper rack. 'Here it is. Young Fern looks like her mother, don't you think?'

Louise looked down at the elegant woman staring back at her. Why hadn't she noticed the resemblance? Fern possessed the same green-blue eyes and strawberry-blonde hair.

'By all accounts, Mr Irons worshipped her.' Mrs Tolley sighed. 'But you know what these supermodels are like — always wanting to be the centre of attention. Life in the country was too dull for her. She craved the bright lights.'

'You mentioned something about a message?' Louise prompted, feeling uncomfortable discussing Charlie's ex-wife behind his back.

'So I did. Miss McDonald said to tell Mr Irons that young Gemma — that's Fern's cousin — will be arriving tomorrow afternoon, and could someone be in to meet her about half past three.'

'That's the time Fern comes home from school.'

'I'll go up to the top of the lane to meet the bus if you like,' Mrs Tolley offered.

'If it wouldn't be too much trouble,' Louise said gratefully.

'No trouble at all. You can't be in two places at the same time, can you?'

★ ★ ★

26

Charlie greeted the news of Gemma's impending arrival with a marked lack of enthusiasm. 'I was hoping Pia's parents would look after her for a few more days.'

'Who exactly is Gemma?' Louise asked.

'She's the daughter of Pia's brother and his wife. They were killed in an accident when Gemma was a baby, and Pia's parents brought her up. After Fern was born, Pia and I thought the two girls would be good company for each other.'

'But surely the situation changed when you and Miss McDonald — I mean . . . ' Louise floundered, not sure of the right words to use.

'Pia and I didn't want to disrupt Fern's life more than was absolutely necessary after we divorced,' Charlie answered her question, 'as Fern's cousin Gemma is part of the family unit. Pia's parents don't find it easy looking after an adolescent girl, so arrangements are made for her to spend some time with them and

27

some time here.'

'Isn't that disruptive to everyone concerned?'

'Fern thinks the world of Gemma,' Charlie replied.

Louise's heart sank. In Charlie-speak that made it a done deal, but from what Louise had heard of Gemma she didn't sound the sort of girl who took kindly to authority.

The next afternoon the sound of a car in the forecourt drew Louise's attention to the window. A uniformed chauffeur stepped smartly out of the driving seat of a sleek limousine. He opened the rear passenger door and stood back to allow the passenger to disembark.

With a fixed smile on her face, Louise went to greet the new arrival.

3

'You must be Gemma. I'm Louise.'

Her welcome was ignored. 'Where's Fern?'

'She isn't back from school yet, but she'll be here shortly.'

'My suitcase is in the back,' Gemma said to no one in particular.

The chauffeur raised his eyes at Louise and made to open the boot. Louise stepped forward and put a hand on his sleeve. 'If you'd like to bring your things into the house, Gemma, we'll start getting tea ready. I'm sure you're hungry after your long journey, and I know Fern will be eager for something to eat.'

The dark brown eyes flickered in her direction, surprise replacing the sulky look on Gemma's face. 'No one gives me orders.'

'Then I suggest you thank . . . ' She turned to the driver. 'I'm sorry, I don't know your name.'

'It's Jim, miss,' he replied.

'That you thank Jim for driving you all the way down here,' Louise said.

'Why should I?'

'Because he's a busy man and he can't waste any more time on you.' Louise's heart was beating a triple tattoo. If Gemma stood her ground, they were in trouble. But to her relief, the girl gave an indifferent shrug.

'Whatever.' She slouched towards the boot, opened it and dragged out an enormous suitcase. 'Thanks, Jim.'

'Any time.' With a smile at Louise, he got back into the car.

'Here,' Gemma said to Louise, 'it's full of my dirty washing.'

'Then you'd better empty it out, hadn't you? I'll show you how to work the machine when I have a spare moment.'

'Who *are* you?' Gemma repeated as if she couldn't quite believe this was actually happening to her.

'Louise Drew. I'm Charlie's personal assistant.'

'You won't be for much longer.'

Battle lines were clearly being drawn. Louise wondered if Gemma was right, and if she had exceeded her authority, before her mother's words rang in her ears: *No one is too young to learn good manners.*

In many ways Gemma reminded Louise of her younger self. When she had been growing up, she and her mother had gone through a difficult phase. Gemma's emotional baggage reminded Louise of her adolescent traumas.

'Thank you for getting your suitcase out of the boot,' Louise said, making an effort to smile. 'Now if you'd like to bring it through, I'll put the kettle on. You can help make the toast.'

If she hadn't been so stressed, Louise would have laughed at the expression on Gemma's face. Leaving the girl standing in the forecourt, she headed for the kitchen. A few moments later she heard suitcase wheels rolling over the cobblestones behind her.

★   ★   ★

'Gemma!' Louise heard the excited shout as she was stirring a saucepan of baked beans.

'Hey, Fern.' Gemma abandoned the toaster and raised a hand to greet her cousin. The two girls slapped palms. Fern giggled.

'I've missed you.'

'Yeh, well, I'm here now.'

Mrs Tolley poked her head through the open door. 'I'll be off then,' she announced. 'If there's nothing else . . . ?'

'Thank you.' Louise waved at the housekeeper, then turned her attention back to Fern and Gemma, who were staring at her in silent unison. 'Hungry?' she asked Fern.

The younger girl looked towards Gemma to take the lead.

Gemma sat down at the table. 'We might be.'

'Wash your hands first, please — both of you. Then the knives and forks are in the drawer. Mrs Tolley's made a special chocolate cake for afterwards.'

Hunger overcame their scruples, and Louise was forced to hide a smile as the two girls tucked into their tea, not wanting to show too much enthusiasm but at the same time clearing their plates.

Gemma pushed back her chair after she'd finished a second slice of Mrs Tolley's cake. 'Upstairs?' she suggested. 'I want to download a new app — it's seriously cool.' Without a glance in Louise's direction, the girls scuttled out of the kitchen.

For the first time since Gemma had been driven into the forecourt, Louise allowed herself to relax. Refreshing the pot of tea, she cut a large wedge of chocolate cake and took a healthy bite.

'Don't scoff the lot,' a voice behind her said, almost making her choke. 'Leave some for me.'

With her mouth full and unable to speak, Louise motioned towards the teapot.

'I'll pour if you cut me a slice of

cake.' Charlie eyed the crumbs on the table and the cooling beans. 'I'll have those too,' he said, and scooped them out of the saucepan. They were gone in two mouthfuls. 'That's better.' He sat down opposite her. 'I take it that Gemma's arrived?'

Louise swallowed her mouthful of cake. 'She's upstairs with Fern now.'

'I'll catch up with them later.' He frowned. 'Gemma's going to be living with us on a semi-permanent basis,' he announced, looking at Louise as if inviting comment. When she remained silent, he continued, 'Pia texted to say she was asked to leave her London school.'

'Did she give a reason?'

'A difference of opinion with her headmistress.'

'That could mean anything.'

'My thoughts entirely.' He drank some of his tea. 'I know it's asking a lot, but I can't look after two growing girls on my own, even if one of them is my daughter.'

'What makes you think I'm an ideal choice for the job?'

'Your rhinoceros hide?'

'You're taking that remark out of context,' Louise retaliated.

'I know, but it was you who threw it in my face and informed me nothing anyone said or did could hurt you, wasn't it?'

Louise couldn't argue with that. Her words came back to haunt her with startling clarity. 'I'll give it my best shot,' she replied.

'Excellent. Anyway, enough of that.' Charlie finished the last of the chocolate cake. 'Good news. I've been down to Selsey — that's on the south coast — and I've managed to source some excellent fresh fish from a supplier who goes out in his own boat most days except when the weather's bad. I've also put out a few feelers regarding farm produce.'

A loud bump followed by the thump of music made them both jump. 'Looks like the girls are getting into their stride,' Louise said.

'I'd better go and make welcoming noises.'

Before she could update him on what had gone on between herself and Gemma so far, he ducked his head to avoid the low beam of the kitchen door and began to climb the stairs. Standing up, Louise began to clear the table. Outside she could hear the workmen finishing up for the day. On the dresser her mobile buzzed.

'Hi, it's Rocko,' a voice greeted her when she answered.

'Where've you been?' Louise demanded.

'Round and about. How's my favourite niece?'

'Fine.'

'I hear you've got yourself a new job.'

Rocko's happy voice always cheered her up. During the dark days following her dismissal from the studio, he had always been there for her. He hadn't criticised anyone or made excuses for what had happened — that wasn't his style — but he had offered a solid shoulder to cry on, a service he had provided many times in Louise's life.

'Fancy a gig to celebrate?' he asked.

'When?'

'Tonight?'

'That's short notice.'

'You can't make it?'

'As long as I'm back by midnight.'

'You're not going to turn into a pumpkin, are you?'

'Hope not,' Louise laughed. 'But seriously, I do have to work tomorrow.'

'You can tell me all the news later. Pick you up at six?'

'Better make it half past. Charlie's been out all day and I need to catch up on one or two things first.'

'Half past it is then, darling. *Ciao.*'

Rocko was the family black sheep. When he'd dropped out of college saying he wanted to take up the guitar for a living, it had caused a serious family rift. He was her father's older brother; and James, Louise's father, had been as scandalised as their parents. James had followed his father into his solicitor's practice and become an established member of the local community. To have a brother who busked and lived in a commune was a step too far, and for a while the brothers had not spoken. Eventually their mother had intervened, and whilst Rocko and James would never be soulmates, they were at least on speaking terms. Their relationship had deepened after James was injured in an accident that had caused him mobility issues. Rocko had been a tower of strength to the family in their time of need, and now they all rubbed along reasonably well together.

* * *

'Who's that?' Gemma asked in an awed voice.

Fern scrambled up onto the window seat beside her and leaned out to get a better look. 'I don't know,' she replied. Gemma pressed her nose to the window.

The girls watched the man ease his wiry frame out of the driving seat of a maintenance van that had seen better days. He stretched his legs; then, catching sight of the two young faces at the window, he winked. Gemma and Fern ducked out of sight with embarrassed giggles.

Rocko threw open his arms and hugged Louise. 'You get more beautiful every time I see you.'

'Rocko,' Louise protested with a laugh, 'you say that to all the girls.'

'But I only mean it when I say it to you,' he insisted.

'You know what? I believe you.'

'Hi, man.' He glanced at Charlie, who was hovering behind Louise's shoulder. 'You treating my girl right?'

'I don't believe we've met,' Charlie said in a frosty voice.

'Rocko Drew, bass guitarist extraordinaire.'

'You play the guitar for a living?'

'I create sound.' He slapped his open palm against Charlie's hand. 'You're the cook?'

Louise bit her lip in an effort not to smile. Being referred to as 'the cook' was hardly the way to refer to a celebrity chef of Charlie's standing.

Charlie's response was a clipped, 'Don't be late back, Louise; we have a busy day tomorrow.'

'I've got my instructions. Midnight, no later, otherwise we're in deep trouble.' The lines on Rocko's lived-in face creased into a smile. 'But everyone deserves some down time, wouldn't you say? And this little lady's had precious little of that recently. So we're going to shoot the breeze.'

Making a noise that sounded suspiciously like a grunt of disbelief, Charlie turned on his heel and headed towards his office.

'Does he have a problem?' Rocko asked.

'He's got a lot on his mind,' Louise replied.

'You know my philosophy: there's no use worrying about things. If they're gonna happen, no worrying in the world is going to stop them.'

With old-fashioned courtesy, he opened the passenger door for Louise and settled her safely on the front seat of the van.

'Shift that wire cable if it's in your way.'

'I can manage,' Louise assured him.

'In that case, let's hit the road. 'Fraid it's only a practice session tonight.'

'They're the best.'

Rocko asked as they trundled along, 'So what's with the cooking? I thought you were done with that scene.'

'Charlie's opening a restaurant, but it's still in the development stages.'

'Hey, it's coming back to me. Wasn't he the guy there was all the fuss about? Grandpa Irons, wasn't that his shout?'

'Do you mind if we don't talk about Charlie or cooking, Rocko?'

'Suits me,' he agreed. 'You know my tastes in cuisine.'

'As long as there are enough eggs and chips on the plate, you're satisfied.'

'Got it in one.'

As they approached the surprisingly luxurious warehouse that Rocko and the rest of the band called home, they could hear music booming out of the speakers. Through the open doors Louise could see flashing lights creating patterns on the walls.

Rocko's van bumped over the grass and came to a halt in front of the double doors. 'Do you need to freshen up first?' he asked.

'No,' Louise assured him, 'I'm raring to go.'

'In that case, the drums are this way. Best stress reliever I know, and we're playing all the old numbers. Do you have your sticks with you?'

'I never travel without them.' Louise produced them from her shoulder bag.

★ ★ ★

By the end of the evening, Louise's arms ached and her head was buzzing. 'That was a blast,' she told Jake, the lead singer, as he turned off his microphone.

'Sure you won't come on the road with us?' he asked. 'We'd have a ball.'

Rocko made a face. 'Don't go putting ideas into her head. Her parents would never speak to me again. And talking of having a ball, I have to get Louise back home.'

'Is that the time?' Louise gasped, glancing at her watch.

'It's only a little past midnight,' Jake protested, 'and we haven't had supper yet.'

'I haven't time for supper. Charlie has an early-morning appointment.'

'Is that the new boss?' Jake asked. 'He sounds like a slave driver to me.'

'He is,' Rocko agreed.

'I really do have to get back,' Louise insisted.

Rocko sketched a bow. 'In that case, your carriage awaits. I know a short cut.'

★ ★ ★

'What's that noise?' Louise asked as the engine began to shudder ten minutes into the journey back to Brooks Farm.

'Not sure,' Rocko replied, 'but nothing to worry about.'

Moments later they glided to a halt.

'Any idea where we are?' Rocko

wound down his window and looked up at the sky as if seeking inspiration from the stars.

'This was your short cut,' Louise pointed out.

'Everything looks different in the dark.'

'What are we going to do?'

'Do you have your mobile?'

'I left it in my other bag. What about you?'

'You know technology is beyond me,' he replied with a cheerful smile.

'So we don't have a mobile on us, we've broken down in the middle of nowhere, and you don't know what's wrong with the van.'

'I have a sneaking suspicion that we've run out of fuel.'

'Rocko . . . ' Louise found it difficult to keep the exasperation out of her voice.

'I know, I know, but I was so excited at the thought of seeing you again that filling up the tank was the last thing on my mind.' He paused. 'There's no sign of rain.'

'Are you suggesting we walk home?'

'It's not far.'

'You said you didn't know where we were.'

'There's only one way to find out.'

It was well past two o'clock, and Louise's feet were seriously sore, by the time they reached Brooks Farm. Rocko had draped his leather jacket around her shoulders in a gesture of gallantry, but even so, she was shivering from the cold night air.

'Told you we'd make it.' Rocko sounded as perky as ever.

Louise's fingers were stiff as she tried to manipulate her door key.

'Are you going to ask me in?'

Before she could reply, the forecourt was bathed in harsh electric light. 'What time do you call this?' Charlie asked, blocking the doorway.

'Hi, man,' Rocko greeted him. 'You don't happen to have a spare can of petrol, do you?'

Twin beams arced across the far wall of the courtyard, and with a loud toot of its horn a sports car throbbed through the open gates.

'It's all happening tonight.' Rocko smiled in the direction of the new arrival.

'Who's that?' Charlie demanded.

'Nothing to do with me,' Rocko insisted, holding up his hands in a gesture of innocence. 'No one I know owns a set of wheels like that.'

Above them a window opened and two excited heads peered out. 'Daddy, there's a car in the forecourt.'

'Go back to bed, Fern,' Charlie bellowed.

'Mummy!' Fern shrieked as a blonde-haired woman emerged from the sports car.

'Hello, darling.' Pia threw her daughter a kiss before her cat-like eyes swept over the trio of individuals grouped in the doorway. 'I didn't expect a reception committee,' she drawled, her eyes lingering on Louise's dishevelled appearance. 'But as no one seems to have gone to bed yet, does anyone fancy a late supper?'

'Bring it on.' Rocko leapt forward with alacrity and, offering his arm, escorted Pia McDonald up the steps and into the kitchen.

4

'He's your uncle?' Charlie said incredulously, nursing his black coffee. 'And Rocko — what sort of name is that?'

'He re-invented himself.'

Charlie cast Louise a disbelieving look. 'At his age?'

'He was a college dropout. And if we're trading home truths about family, I could point out that it was your ex-wife who insisted he stay on until the all-night garage delivered a can of petrol.'

'He didn't have to make a party of it.'

'Rocko makes a party of everything, and that's why I love him so much. And if you continue like this, I'm walking out of that door right now.'

Charlie gave her a shamefaced smile. 'Your job's safe and no one's going anywhere.' He sipped some coffee. 'Actually, hold that. You're going somewhere.'

'I am?'

'Because we overslept, Gemma and Fern have missed the bus. You're going to have to do the school run.'

'Gemma's going to school with Fern?'

'Pia's made all the arrangements.'

'Then shouldn't she be the one to deliver the girls?'

'Pia doesn't do mornings well, especially not when she's had a late night — correction, an early morning. She'll sleep until lunch time.' Charlie stifled a yawn. 'What time did you actually get to bed?'

'I'm not sure,' admitted Louise, wishing she too could have stayed in bed longer, 'but I think the sun was up.'

Charlie slammed down his mug 'Right — we need to get on with the day. Things to do.'

'Where are the girls now?'

'I'm here,' Fern said as she raced in, her blouse half-undone and tie askew. 'Can I have toast soldiers?'

'There isn't time,' Charlie said as he poured some cereal into a bowl. 'Hurry up and eat this. Where's Gemma?'

'In the bathroom.'

Charlie raised an eyebrow at Louise. 'I think you'd better deal with that one.'

'On my way,' she said with little enthusiasm. Another encounter with Gemma this early in the morning was not the best way to set up the day.

'Gemma?' Louise called through the door. 'We're ready to leave.'

The door swung open. 'Then let's go,' Gemma said.

Louise stepped back in surprise. 'You're not going to school like that,' she gasped.

Gemma was wearing denim shorts over black tights, a huge blue T-shirt with the logo of a boy band printed on the front, a red jacket and a brown fedora. There was a suggestion of mascara on her eyelashes and the faintest trace of lipstick.

'I don't have a uniform. These are the only clean clothes I have.'

'Fine,' Louise gave in without a fight. She decided this was something Charlie and Pia could deal with.

Disappointment flared in Gemma's eyes. 'You mean it's okay?'

50

'We're leaving in five minutes,' Louise said, ignoring her question. 'If you want any breakfast, Fern's eating hers in the kitchen now.'

'Where are you going?' Gemma called after her.

'To take a shower.'

If Louise was going to have to explain the situation to the head teacher, it wouldn't do to look as though she had spent half the night drumming with a rock band and the other half partying in Charlie's kitchen until the small hours. A quick shower revived her flagging senses, and she was back down in the kitchen in record time. There was no sign of Gemma. A disgruntled Fern was kicking her heels against her chair, a rebellious look on her face.

'It's swimming today and I haven't got my things.'

Charlie looked up from inspecting a schedule on his clipboard. 'I have to see to the builders. Can you deal with it, Louise? I've done the dishes.'

'Where's Mrs Tolley?' she asked.

'Day off.' He flashed a dazzling smile. 'Know you can cope.' He raced out of the door, leaving a fuming Louise staring after him.

*   *   *

Not caring if Brooks Farm was in a state of utter chaos, Louise stopped off in town on her drive back from Fern's school. Mrs Young, the head teacher, had been very understanding about their late arrival and Gemma's fashion choice, but had insisted that she wear regulation uniform as soon as conveniently possible.

Before he'd left in the small hours, Rocko had slipped some money into Louise's pocket. 'Treat yourself to something nice,' he insisted.

'Rocko, no.' Louise tried to hand it back.

'I'll be seriously offended if I hear you haven't squandered every penny. Now where's that petrol?' He looked round for the can. 'What was that for?'

he asked as Louise kissed his cheek.

'No reason.'

'Then I'll have another one,' he said with a grin.

Now Louise decided to head for the hairdresser. Working in a television studio had meant that the services of hairdressers, make-up artists and every available beauty product were readily available. Her shoulder-length blonde hair was regularly trimmed and conditioned. But since her ignominious departure, she hadn't bothered to have it cut, and it was now sorely in need of treatment.

The door to the hairdressers pinged as she pushed it open. She inhaled the smell of exotic shampoos and beauty lotions. Then, hoping for a cancellation, she headed towards the glamorous receptionist.

Ten minutes later she was leaning back in the padded treatment chair. After a quick consultation with the stylist, who tutted over the state of her hair, Louise relaxed while the junior massaged a lavender-and-mint intensive treatment into her scalp. Apart from her daily shower, she couldn't remember the last time she had actually bothered to condition her hair.

'How's the pressure?' the junior asked.

'Mm,' Louise answered, nearly falling asleep, 'lovely.'

A warm towel was wrapped around her head, and Louise allowed herself to be moved to another padded seat while a second assistant massaged the back of her shoulders.

The stylist inspected the ends of Louise's hair. 'It needs a good cut. Some of the ends are split.'

It was an hour and a half before Louise was ready to emerge from the beauty salon. 'The style will be much easier to handle,' the stylist said. 'And the shorter length suits you.'

A quick glance in the mirror assured Louise that she hadn't been subjected to some clever marketing. The assistants had gone a good job. She headed back to Brooks Farm in a more confident frame of mind.

She barely had time to get out of the

car before Charlie descended on her. 'Where have you been?' he demanded. 'And what have you done to your hair?'

'There you are,' Pia said, teetering towards her on impossibly high heels. Her eyes narrowed as she took in Louise's new hairdo. 'You're not paid to spend all day in the beauty parlour.'

'Leave this to me, Pia,' Charlie insisted.

'You needn't think anyone will notice,' Pia sneered.

'Charlie did.' Louise tempered her words with a cheerful smile.

'Now that you're back,' Charlie intervened, 'perhaps you'd make some tea for the builders?'

'I'll have a cup too, please.' Pia turned on her heel. 'China, with a slice of lemon. No milk. Bring it to my bedroom.'

'Couldn't Pia have made the tea?' Louise hissed as soon as she was out of earshot, and thinking of the pile of paperwork Charlie had thrust at her earlier in the week.

'She's promised to take care of the telephone.'

'And what are you going to do?'

'I've been given the name of a new contact regarding dairy produce. Today is the only time we can meet up. You've got my number if there are any emergencies.'

Louise found Pia lying on her bed flipping through the pages of a magazine.

'I was beginning to wonder what had happened to you.'

'It takes time to brew a pot of builders' tea.'

'Well, I'm sure you're used to doing that sort of thing. You were junior third assistant in your little studio, weren't you?'

Louise gritted her teeth, determined not to retaliate.

Pia inspected her manicure. 'I must get my nails done. They're in a dreadful state.' The telephone interrupted them. 'Get that, would you? I'm absolutely exhausted. It's been ringing non-stop all morning while you've been gallivanting around the countryside. By the way, what's the name of the beauty parlour you went to? I might pay them a visit later.'

Ignoring the pounding in her head, Louise retreated to the office and tried desperately to remember all Charlie's instructions regarding the spreadsheet he wanted setting up. All telephone calls had been switched through to the main house for Pia to answer, but it wasn't until one of the workmen poked his head round the door of the office that Louise realised it was half past three and the girls would soon be home from school.

'Here's a list of your messages,' he said with a cheerful smile.

'Messages?'

'Mrs Irons said we were to answer any calls that came through to the kitchen after she went out.'

'How long has she been gone?' Louise demanded.

'About an hour. We're off for the day. See you tomorrow.'

Feeling sick, Louise raced over to the

farmhouse. More notes scrawled in green ink had been pinned on the corkboard in a haphazard fashion. One or two had come loose and floated to the floor. As Louise bent down to pick them up, she heard the sound of a car outside.

A dapper man in a striped blazer and wearing a spotted bow tie knocked on the back door. 'Mrs Irons?'

'It's Miss Drew, actually,' Louise replied, quickly altering the annoyed expression on her face to one of polite enquiry. 'What can I do for you?'

'My name's Quentin Voisin.' He paused expectantly. 'Cookery writer?'

Louise froze. 'Mr Irons said you were due on Friday.'

'Didn't you get my message?' Quentin frowned in annoyance. 'Your assistant promised to pass it on.' He looked down at the note Louise had retrieved from the floor and placed on the table. 'Here it is.' He snatched it up.

'I'm sorry, but there seems to have been a lapse in communication. I wasn't expecting you.'

'This isn't good enough,' he tutted. 'But now I'm here, we might as well get on with things.'

'I don't understand.'

'As you can read from this note,' Quentin said, waving Pia's scrap of paper under Louise's nose, 'due to a last-minute change of plans, I find myself available to do my piece today. So if there are no further objections, I'd like to look round.'

'Mr Irons isn't here.'

'This really is too bad.' He now sounded like a spoilt child denied a treat.

'If there's anything I can do . . . ' Louise offered.

'I very much doubt it.' He looked her up and down. The telephone sprang into life again. 'Hadn't you better answer that?' he suggested. 'You don't want another missed message.'

Louise did so and was greeted with, 'Miss Drew? This is Mrs Young here.'

'Is there a problem at the school?'

Louise asked, realising it was now well past four o'clock and there was no sign of Fern or Gemma.

'I need to contact Mr Irons immediately as a matter of extreme urgency.'

'He's out at the moment.'

'Then Mrs Irons will do.'

'She's also unavailable. What's wrong? Have the girls had an accident?'

'Gemma sneaked out of school during the lunch break. No one realised she was missing because she was only registered today. Fern was in swimming class, otherwise I'm sure her absence would have been noticed earlier. I have Gemma in my office now. Can you come over? The girls have missed the bus home.'

Louise hurriedly ended the call and said to Quentin, 'I have to go out.' She snatched car keys off the hook.

'Go out?' he spluttered.

'There's a crisis at the school.'

'And what am I supposed to do?'

'You could come with me,' she suggested.

'I could not. I've gone to great

trouble rearranging my schedule to be here today.'

'In that case,' Louise said, only half-listening, 'if you want to look round, feel free. Lock up before you leave, would you? You can post the keys through the letterbox.'

Louise raced out of the kitchen, leaving the outraged critic lost for words.

5

'What was I supposed to do?' Louise was so incensed that she had difficulty keeping her voice steady. 'Pia had gone out. You weren't here. I had no idea Quentin had changed his schedule.'

'You could've thought of something.'

'I did. I offered him the option of coming with me.'

Charlie smacked a hand to his forehead in disbelief. 'Is that the best you could come up with?'

'I was thinking on my feet. What would you have done?' Louise knew she was shouting, but she didn't seem to be getting through to Charlie. 'Your daughter and niece missed the bus home from school. Don't you care that Gemma was wandering around the town and no one realised she was missing?'

'Of course I care, but that's not the point.'

'I think it is. I dread to think what might have happened to her if one of the teachers hadn't spotted her.'

'Is this some kind of revenge?'

'Now what are you talking about?'

'Quentin Voisin has the power to make or break people in this industry. If you wanted to do a hatchet job on my reputation, you've succeeded.'

'How dare you.' Louise had now reached boiling point.

'Keep it down, guys,' Pia said as she strolled into the kitchen and, picking a strawberry out of the fruit bowl, nibbled on the ripe fruit. She licked the juice from her lips, her feline eyes absorbing every detail of the unfolding drama.

She reminded Louise of a cat indulging in a lavish dish of cream. Her nails had been freshly manicured, and she had obviously been on a spending spree. The dress she was wearing emphasised her figure, clinging in all the right places, making Louise feel frumpier than ever in her practical leggings and loose work shirt. She thrust open the window; Pia's perfume was overpowering.

'The girls are playing a video game. Do you think you could make them some tea, Louise, and leave the argument until later?'

Louise ignored Pia and addressed Charlie. 'Would you like to repeat what you just said?'

'What?' He blinked in confusion.

'Forgotten already? Then let me refresh your memory. As I understand it, you accused me of arranging for Gemma to abscond from school in order to sabotage your interview with Quentin Voisin.'

'That isn't what I said.' He was now very red in the face.

'It sounded like that to me.'

'And it sounds to me as though you've lost it, Louise,' Pia edged in to the exchange.

'Stay out of this please,' Charlie clipped back at her.

Pia's mouth tightened in annoyance. 'I will not — and if the pair of you would do me the courtesy of listening to what I have to say instead of hurling accusations across the kitchen, we can clear this matter up in moments. Thank you.' Pia acknowledged the silence that had fallen between Charlie and Louise. 'I left a note for you, Louise,' she continued, 'telling you about Quentin's change of schedule, which you failed to pick up.'

'You could've delivered it personally. I was only across the forecourt.'

'I was late for an important appointment.'

'With your manicurist?'

Pia's eyes glinted like shards of steel. 'I hold you fully responsible for what happened, and if Charlie's got any sense, he should sue you for the professional damage you've caused.'

'Steady on, Pia. There's no need to go that far,' Charlie cautioned.

'I've had my say.' She shrugged.

Through the open door, Louise heard the sound of laughter floating down from the bedroom Fern shared with Gemma. She flinched as Millie the cat flicked her tail down the side of her legs, meowing plaintively. Louise filled a saucer from the milk carton on the table, placed it on the floor and watched the tabby lap it up, all the while not trusting herself to speak.

'No one's suggesting we take legal action.' Charlie began to look uncomfortable with his ex-wife's choice of words.

Louise found her voice. 'It wouldn't get you anywhere if you did. I don't have a penny to my name; but if you want to sue, go right ahead.'

'Why don't we talk about this later when everyone's had a chance to cool down?' Charlie suggested.

'I don't need to calm down,' Pia said, fiddling with one of her earrings. 'But why don't you take a walk around the courtyard, Louise? It might help to clear your head.'

Louise took a deep breath and counted to five. 'Charlie,' she said, her voice firm and in control, 'you need to speak to Gemma.'

'If there's any speaking to be done to

'my niece, I'll see to it, thank you,' Pia insisted.

'It was because of Gemma that the girls missed the school bus home.'

'Hardly a serious offence, but I'll speak to the girls in my own time,' Pia replied.

'There's more,' Louise battled on.

'If you don't mind, I have several calls to make.' Pia was beginning to sound bored.

'Fine. I'll leave you to deal with things, Pia.' Charlie made for the door. 'I'll be in the restaurant if anyone needs me.'

Louise's self-control snapped. 'For heaven's sake, don't either of you care about Gemma?' Her mobile chose that moment to ring. She watched in dismay as Pia, following Charlie's example, swept out of the kitchen.

'Mum?' Her jaw was aching with tension as she registered the caller identity. 'Can I call you back?'

'It's your father.'

'I'm on my way.'

Not caring if Charlie took her to court for vehicle theft, Louise threw a few things into her overnight bag then grabbed the car keys. Within ten minutes she was on her way. Stopping off at a service station, she made another quick call to her mother.

'Darling, where are you?' Peggy Drew sounded worried.

'Half way down the motorway. I should be with you in an hour.'

'Drive carefully,' she warned her daughter.

'How's Dad?'

'We'll talk when you get here.'

The light was fading as Louise drew up outside her parents' north London Victorian terraced house. It was down the end of a tree-lined cul-de-sac, and Peggy was looking out for her.

'You look exhausted.' She put an arm around Louise's shoulders and ushered her daughter inside.

'Don't fuss,' Louise insisted.

'I'm your mother; it's my job to fuss.'

'Where's Dad?

'Resting in the other room. Best not to disturb him.'

'What happened?'

'He had a slight fall up at the allotment — nothing serious — but he wasn't discovered for an hour or so. The doctor's advised him to rest up for the next few days, but you know your father.'

Ever since he had taken early retirement, James Drew had refused to give in to his health issues. He liked to keep active and independent, and his allotment was his pride and joy. Vegetables were his speciality, and his flowers had won rosettes.

'I've made some tea, and there's some leftover coffee gateau in the fridge.'

'I'm not hungry,' Louise insisted.

'Yes you are.' Her mother was equally insistent. 'Sit down while I pour the tea.'

Louise began to nibble on the soft sponge. Apart from half a slice of toast snatched over the breakfast table, she had eaten nothing all day, and she soon realised her mother was right. She was ravenous.

Peggy replaced the teapot on the stand and looked expectantly at her daughter.

'What's wrong?' Peggy asked.

'Nothing's wrong.' She addressed her attention to her slice of cake, not looking her mother in the face.

'You're not ill?'

'No,' Louise said.

'You're not in any other sort of trouble?' Peggy probed. 'Money, personal problems?'

'No, nothing like that.'

'Then in your own good time,' she said in the tone of voice she used when she wanted answers.

A wave of shame swept over Louise. She had used her mother's call to flee Brooks Farm, when the proper course of action to take would have been to tough it out with Charlie. So what if Quentin gave them a rotten review or no review at all? It wasn't the end of the world.

'I don't know where to start.' Louise realised she had been foolish to think she could fool her mother.

'I can hear your father stirring.' Peggy cocked an ear. 'I'd better go and see to him.'

Louise stood up and looked out of the French windows. She should have made Pia and Charlie listen to her. Gemma's actions were a cry for help, and she had let the girl down. Louise sighed. Ever since she had lost her job at the studio, she had been guilty of muddled thinking. Today she had surpassed herself, taking a car she didn't own and disappearing without a word to anyone. She knew she should contact Charlie to explain, but right now she didn't think either of them was in the mood to listen to each other.

Her father's rose garden was now silhouetted against the evening dusk, and the sight of it never failed to revive her jaded spirits. 'Much better than sitting in a stuffy office,' James had confided to Louise on one of his better days when the two of them had been enjoying an afternoon's gardening.

'Hello, darling. It's lovely to see you. Sorry I've been such a nuisance.'

Louise swung round at the sound of a voice behind her and watched her father leaning heavily on his stick, limping towards her. Fiercely independent, he did not welcome assistance, and Louise smiled back at him as he made his way across the room and settled down in his favourite armchair.

'You could never be a nuisance,' Louise insisted, 'except when you try to do too much.' Her father eyed up the remains of the coffee cake, and she lowered her voice to a whisper. 'I won't tell if you have a slice.'

'I know I shouldn't, but I never could resist your mother's baking.'

Louise handed him a clean plate and watched him cut himself a generous slice. 'So what have you been up to?' he asked as he settled back in his chair.

'I saw Rocko the other day.'

James pulled a face. 'Is he still

playing that dreadful guitar?'

''Fraid so, and don't let him hear you call his beloved master a dreadful guitar.'

'Why not? I've called it everything else,' James replied with a spark of old spirit.

'He asked after you.'

'That was kind of him, I hope you told him I was well?'

'I did.'

'I know he's my brother and all that, but I don't suppose I'll ever understand him or his lifestyle.'

'That's what makes families special.' Louise smiled indulgently. 'If you've finished your cake, why don't I hide the evidence?'

James yawned. 'Good idea.' He passed over his plate. 'I think I'll have another nap before dinner. Lovely to see you again. Give me a hug before I settle down on the sofa.'

Louise found her mother slicing tomatoes in the kitchen. 'Let me help.' She took the vegetable knife from

Peggy. 'You could join Dad in the lounge if you like.'

Her mother peered through the serving hatch. 'He's asleep. I won't disturb him. I thought we'd have soup, an omelette and salad?'

'Sounds delicious.'

Peggy began whisking up the eggs in a mixing bowl. 'So — Charlie Irons?' she asked in an overly casual voice.

Louise filled a saucepan with water. 'What about him?'

'Is there too much baggage between you for things to be a success?'

'He can be temperamental,' Louise replied. With her unerring instinct for the truth, Peggy had put her finger on the heart of the problem.

'That's one thing you have in common,' Peggy acknowledged with a smile.

'I'm not temperamental,' Louise protested.

'You're ambitious, stubborn and a perfectionist, and that makes you picky.'

'If I am, then they're qualities I inherited from you.'

'I've never given up on anything.' Peggy directed a pointed look at her daughter.

'I think Charlie Irons has given up on me,' Louise replied in a quiet voice.

'The politics of the situation aren't important.' Peggy held up a hand before Louise could explain what had happened. 'Don't be afraid to back down, Louise. He won't think any the worse of you.'

'I wasn't in the wrong.'

'Then you'll earn his respect.'

'You mean I'll have the moral high ground?'

'He'll owe you one, Louise. Isn't that how it's said these days?'

Louise kissed her mother's cheek. 'You're a very clever woman. Thanks for listening to my nonsense.'

Peggy turned her attention back to the eggs. 'Are these fluffy enough?'

'No one makes an omelette like you do.'

'Right. Then why don't you take a shower before we eat? There's plenty of time.'

Upstairs in her old bedroom, Louise dropped her holdall onto the floor. Her mother had placed a sprig of lavender on her pillow next to a freshly laundered nightdress. Louise brushed the delicate sprig over her cheek, enjoying the sensation of calm it invoked. Placing it carefully back on her pillow, she bent down, heaved her bag onto the bed and unzipped it.

Fern's swimming things fell out. As Louise picked up the damp towel in annoyance, an assortment of CDs, make-up, and several pieces of costume jewellery, all with the price tags still attached, landed on the bed.

6

'No, she isn't with me,' Rocko said over Charlie's mobile.

'Then where is she?' the chef demanded.

'Man, the last time I saw my lovely Louise, she was partying at yours. Are you telling me you've lost her?' Rocko chuckled.

'She left and didn't say where she was going.'

'Family trait I've been guilty of myself.' Rocko was still sounding supremely unconcerned.

'And she's taken one of our cars.'

'She's not a thief. She'll turn up, but she must've been mighty mad to split. Have you been giving her grief?'

'No, I haven't.' Charlie raked a hand through his hair.

'Something must've made her take off without a word,' reasoned Rocko. 'She doesn't usually turn tail without a

77

fight. She's spunky, is my Louise.'

'Spunky or not, she's gone.'

'Then you must've spooked her.'

'I didn't do anything.'

'I'm not sure I believe you, man; and if I knew where she was, which I don't, I wouldn't tell you.'

'Why not?'

'The celebrity chef thing isn't my scene, but like all the other big hitters I've come across in my time, I'm guessing you have a monster ego. Bet my Louise is cutting you down to size. Power to her elbow.'

'This is getting us nowhere.' Charlie's patience with Rocko was wearing thin. 'Do you really not know where Louise is?'

'You have the word of a Drew. Let me know when you find her. I'm kind of fond of Louise. She's my only niece. Peace and love.'

The line went dead.

'He hung up on me.' Charlie stared at Pia in disbelief.

'I'm not surprised. He's probably as

disgusted as I am over her behaviour. Really, I should've thought girls of her age were past having tantrums.'

'It was more than that. We virtually threatened to sue her. No one with any spirit is going to take that lying down.'

'I seem to recall it was you who did the threatening.' Pia's eyes narrowed.

'Let's not go into all that now. The bottom line is, she's gone.'

'Well, you're going to have to come up with some solution to the problem. I'm scheduled for a photo shoot in Venice tomorrow and I have a zillion things to do before my flight leaves.'

'You're going where?'

'Don't you ever listen to anything I say?'

'You can't leave.'

'I have no choice. I'm a professional, and I don't walk out on a job without a word to anyone.'

'Who's going to look after the girls?'

Pia shrugged. 'You'll have to find another assistant, preferably one who doesn't hightail off at the sniff of a crisis. Why you employed that girl in the first place, I'm at a loss to understand. She obviously can't be trusted. I mean, she was the one who stole your job, wasn't she?'

'We all know why I lost my job,' Charlie said in a quiet voice.

Discomfited, Pia fluttered her long eyelashes and fiddled with her hair. 'Don't go there, please.'

'Agreed.' Charlie gave a curt nod of his head. 'The less said the better.'

'You were horrible to her,' a small voice interrupted them. Both pairs of eyes swivelled to the doorway. 'That's why she ran away.'

'Fern?' Charlie was the first to speak.

'You should be in bed.' Pia frowned at her daughter.

'I'm hungry.'

'You had a substantial salad for your tea,' her mother said.

'Louise makes things on toast.'

'Then it's just as well she's not here. Doesn't anyone read my nutrition sheet?'

'Do we need one?' Charlie enquired.

'I do know a fair bit about the subject.'

Fern hid a toothy smile behind her hand. 'Louise is brilliant at drawing patterns with the baked beans,' she said.

'I'm glad there's something she's good at,' Pia drawled.

'It wasn't Gemma's fault,' Fern now insisted, looking at her father.

'What wasn't?' He frowned in confusion.

'Louise doesn't know about it, so you're not to blame her either. We shouldn't have done it,' she said in a rush.

'Done what?' Pia sounded irritated with her daughter.

'Fern, come and sit down.' Charlie drew out a chair. 'Tell us what all this is about.'

Fern scuttled across the kitchen. 'Can I have a biscuit please?'

'You know the rules. No carbs after six,' Pia began. 'Those things are full of E-numbers.'

'The pink wafers are my favourites.' Fern peered into the tin Charlie thrust under her nose.

'When you're ready.' Pia tapped her

81

painted nails on the dresser. 'We don't have all night.'

'Gemma didn't mean to take those things, but she didn't have any money,' Fern explained. 'They're very pretty, and she likes pretty things.'

'Are you saying Gemma stole something?' Charlie spoke slowly.

'That's why we missed the school bus and why Louise came to fetch us. We were in the head teacher's office. Mrs Young was very cross with Gemma. She wrote a letter to you. Gemma sneaked it off her desk when she wasn't looking.'

'Has Gemma been accused of something?' Pia demanded.

'Gemma was going to confess, but then you began shouting at Louise and being horrible to her, and she got scared.'

'I think we'd better hear the full story from Gemma,' Charlie said.

'You're not to bully the child,' Pia told him, grabbing his arm to stop him from leaving the room. 'You won't get any answers from her if you lose your cool.'

'Where's Gemma now?' Charlie tried

to shake Pia's hand off his sleeve.

'Wait a minute,' Pia said, clinging on. 'There's no sense in flying off the handle before we know the full story. Now, Fern, what else can you tell us? And we want the truth, mind. You can start with the letter. What's that all about?'

'Gemma hid it in Louise's things,' Fern explained, crumbling her pink wafer into a mess. 'Mrs Young was cross because neither you nor Daddy came to collect us. Where were you?'

'Stick to the point,' Pia said.

'Gemma wrapped everything up in my damp swimming costume and towel, then hid it all in Louise's bag so you wouldn't find it,' Fern explained patiently.

'Hiding things in someone else's bag isn't a very nice thing to do,' Charlie said.

'I know,' Fern mumbled, looking at the floor. 'But we thought it wouldn't matter because you don't like Louise very much, and I was telling Gemma what fun it was getting her into trouble. You know, doing naughty things and watching her get the blame?' Her eyelashes fluttered nervously as she saw the expression on her father's face.

'Go on,' he urged in a quiet voice.

'We heard Mummy and Louise having an argument.'

'We weren't arguing,' Pia said.

'You were being horrid to her.'

Behind her spectacles, Fern's green-blue eyes mirrored her mother's, but there the resemblance ended. Fern lacked her mother's classic features. The stubborn expression on her face matched that of her father as she crossed her arms and stood her ground in the face of her mother's displeasure.

'Get on with your story,' Pia snapped.

'Louise saw us on the landing. When we asked her where she was going, she said she'd received an urgent call.'

'Do you know anything about this?' Charlie asked Pia.

'First I've heard of it.'

'Louise left the door to her room open,' Fern continued, 'so when she wasn't looking we crept back along the landing and spied on her. She was tipping her night things into a bag.' Her lower lip wobbled.

'Go on,' Charlie coaxed. 'We're not cross with you.'

'When she disappeared into the bathroom, Gemma slipped into her room and stuffed the things she'd taken in her bag, including the letter from Mrs Young. She thought if no one could find the evidence, they couldn't blame her for anything.'

'You didn't speak to Louise again?' her father asked.

'No.'

'She didn't give you any idea where she was going?'

Fern shook her head. 'I wasn't very nice to Louise either, and I'd like to say I'm sorry.' She was now bright red in the face. 'I want her back. She sings funny songs in the car, and she promised us we can go and visit her Uncle Rocko, and she's going to teach us to play the drums. She's got her own drumsticks. Isn't that awesome?'

The only sound to break the ensuing silence was a loud purring noise from Millie, who surveyed the proceedings from her usual spot on the window ledge.

'That girl is never coming back here,' Pia eventually spoke through clenched teeth.

'I don't know. I've always fancied having a go on the drums myself. I should imagine it's great for blowing away the blues.' Charlie mimed a few movements with his hands. Fern clapped in delight.

'What's wrong with the pair of you? We have a serious situation here, and all you can do is pretend to play the drums.'

'Any suggestions as to what we *should* be doing?' Charlie enquired.

'You should be out looking for Louise, that's what. She's absconded with important evidence.'

'Where do we start? Perhaps you'd like to lead the way.'

'Heavens, is that the time?' Pia glanced at her watch in relief as the telephone began to ring. 'I expect it's my agent wondering where I am. Listen out for my taxi, there's an angel, Fern.'

'Where are you going?' Charlie called after her.

'I need to pack. *Ciao*.'

'What about Gemma?'

'Use your charm. Speak to the school. Get her reinstated.'

Fern stood on tiptoe and reached up to take the telephone out of its cradle when it rang. 'Hello?' she said in a polite voice, then broke into a beaming smile. 'Louise!' she squealed, jumping up and down with excitement.

Charlie crossed the floor in one bound and yanked the telephone out of his daughter's hand. Fern, taking advantage of the situation, slipped underneath his raised arms, grabbed a handful of biscuits and scurried upstairs.

'Louise, where are you?' Before she could speak, he said, 'We've been going out of our minds with worry.'

'I'm okay, and I'm sorry I took the car.'

'Never mind about that.'

'Charlie, there's something I have to tell you.'

Fern sneaked back into the kitchen and tugged his sleeve.

'Not now, Fern.'

'Ask her if she's found anything in her bag,' she said in a loud whisper.

'I know this sounds silly,' Charlie spoke slowly and carefully, 'but have you unpacked yet?'

'Yes.'

'Fern says she put her swimming things in your bag.'

'It wasn't me, it was Gemma,' Fern spoke in an indignant voice.

'That's not all she put in my bag. Charlie, Gemma's been shoplifting. I've got the evidence to prove it. I also found a letter from the head teacher. She's been indefinitely suspended.'

'What?'

'The flap wasn't sealed and I read the contents.'

'Why has she been suspended?'

'Because the teacher who found Gemma told Mrs Young she was about to pocket a lipstick. Charlie, it sounds serious. I found make-up, nail varnish, hair products, things like that. Are you still there?' Louise demanded when there was no response.

'Yes, I'm still here.'

'What do you want me to do?'

'I know it's a big ask . . . ' His voice took on a gruff note. ' . . . but can you come back as soon as possible?'

Fern jumped up and down in delight. 'Louise is coming back!' She thudded up the stairs to break the good news to Gemma.

'I don't want to put pressure on you, Louise, but you've got my car,' Charlie wheedled.

'Do you intend to sue me for theft as well as for damages?'

'That remark was made in the heat of the moment,' Charlie snapped.

'Where's Pia?'

'She's flying out to Venice in the morning.' Charlie began to sound desperate. 'Louise, I can't handle this on my own.'

'Did Gemma tell you what happened?'

'Fern gave me her version of events, but I'm not too clear as to exact details. That's why we need to talk.'

Pia's high heels clicked on the kitchen flooring. 'There's my taxi now. I've said goodbye to the girls. I hope things will be sorted by the time I get back.'

Charlie turned his attention back to the telephone after Pia's taxi had departed. 'Louise? I've got a roof terrace flat. It was where I used to crash out after I'd been filming late or wanted to be on my own. It's not far from here. We could meet up there, if you can't face Brooks Farm?'

Louise heard her father's voice float up the stairs. 'How long is Louise staying?' he asked in a sleepy voice as Peggy began to lay the table for supper.

'Ssh, she'll hear you.'

'I don't like my routine disturbed,' he grumbled.

Louise eyed the spoils of Gemma's

shoplifting spree spread out on her bed, then picked up a pen. 'What's the post code of this flat of yours?' she asked.

7

The back of Louise's neck ached with tension as she drew up outside Charlie's flat late in the evening of the following day. She caught a whiff of aftershave as he tightened his arms around her body.

'I've been waiting hours.'

'I couldn't rush off until I'd had some time with my parents.' She tried to wriggle free from his embrace.

'I'm glad you're back.' His blue eyes penetrated Louise's as he eased his hold. 'I'm doing a barbecue on the roof terrace. Let's go on up.'

'Where do you want me to put this?' She indicated the bag at her feet.

'Is that the loot?' Charlie asked with a wry smile.

'It is, and I wouldn't want to be found in possession of stolen goods.'

He picked up the bag and stowed it

behind the front door. 'It can stay there for the time being.'

'Shouldn't we deal with it now?'

'All in good time,' Charlie insisted. 'And it's not going anywhere, is it?'

'I suppose not,' Louise was forced into reluctant agreement. She wished she didn't feel quite so pleased to see Charlie again. He seemed to have made an effort with his appearance. His hair had been trimmed and he was wearing a smart polo shirt and chinos.

'If you're ready?' he prompted.

'Yes, of course.' Louise knew she must pull herself together and remember this was the man who rarely believed a word she said and had actually threatened to take her to court.

'It's this way. Watch your footing. The floor is uneven in places.'

They clambered up a crooked flight of stairs that led out onto a raised decked rooftop. In the corner, smoke billowed from a purpose-built barbecue.

'Make yourself comfortable,' Charlie said. He indicated the colourful sun loungers ranged around the sunken roof garden. 'Would you like some fruit cordial?'

'Please.'

He caught her appreciative look as she took in her surroundings. 'I come up here as often as I can. The world seems a saner place when you're up on the roof. I suppose it's because the people down below look like scurrying ants. All your problems seem to shrink too.'

'What's that lovely smell?' Louise perched on a purple cushion and swung herself to and fro in one of the revolving pod-shaped swing chairs.

'My herb garden. Most of them come out to play at dusk.' He gave a self-conscious smile. 'Unless of course you're referring to the barbecue. I've a couple of ears of corn slow-baking in foil.'

Louise sipped her cordial. The last ten minutes of her drive had been an unpleasant experience: nose to tail with the car in front, and with impatient drivers hooting their horns at every opportunity, she had been more than glad to turn into the mews complex.

'I try to keep the garden as green as possible,' Charlie explained. 'I read somewhere it's important to get the right balance — you know, organic with a bit of smoke.'

Louise nodded, uncertain what to make of Charlie's behaviour. He was certainly trying to be pleasant, but how long would it last? 'Have you had the flat long?' she asked.

'I got it at a knockdown price about eighteen months ago. It was always at the back of my mind to do something with it, then one day I had a lightbulb moment and decided there had to be more to life than sitting in a stifling studio all day, cooking food under hot spotlights. When I caught myself shouting at a make-up girl who hadn't done anything wrong, I knew I needed to get out into the real world. To be honest, I was growing disenchanted with the lifestyle, and my personal life was getting on top of me. If you hadn't come along when you did, I probably would've thrown in the towel anyway. So after I was let go, I started my renovation plan in earnest. I have to admit, the rooftop is the best place to be on a summer's evening.'

He offered Louise an olive. 'Try one of these and let me know what you think. I've sourced an outlet that's given me a competitive quote. They have a contact in Greece, and I've been assured they can meet our demands.'

Louise chose an almond-stuffed green olive. 'It's good,' she said with a nod.

'Then you can add their details to the list. You are coming back, aren't you?'

'Quentin Voisin?' Louise queried.

Charlie shook his head. 'He's history — far too full of his own importance. I don't know why we made such a fuss about him.'

'That's not what you were saying yesterday.'

'I said a lot of things I'm not proud of yesterday,' Charlie admitted. 'Why don't I update you quickly on all that's happened? Then we can get on with enjoying our evening.'

Louise's heartbeat kicked into overdrive. The next few minutes could decide her future.

'Refill?' Charlie held up the jug of cordial.

'Thank you.'

'Right. Gemma. She's Pia's brother's child.'

'I know.'

'Until now she's been living with her grandparents, Pia's mother and father. She comes to stay with Fern and me during the holidays. The trouble is, I think she feels she doesn't really belong anywhere, and so to make her mark she does things to draw attention to herself.'

'What sorts of things?'

'Last summer one Sunday afternoon a group of us went walking in the country. Gemma left all the gates open. Luckily my companion noticed what she was up to and we were able to avert a disaster, but it could've been nasty.'

'I see.'

'I also suspect she's jealous of Fern.'

'Is that why she leads Fern on?'

'You noticed that?' Charlie nodded. 'Unfortunately, Tim and Carol, Pia's parents, are very active in the local community and they don't have as much time or energy to give her as they'd like. Pia's frequently away, so I've sort of inherited her. I don't mind having her stay with us, but I find her presence very taxing, especially at the moment with so much else going on in my life.'

'Have you been in touch with the school?'

'Mrs Young? Yes. She's the mother of teenage daughters, and understands their needs and problems and the changes they're going through. She's agreed to take Gemma back, subject to conditions.'

'What about Fern?'

'She wants to know when you'll be available to draw more pictures with baked beans — a talent I have to admit I didn't know you possessed.'

Louise gave a shamefaced smile. 'It was only a bit of fun, really.'

'I've got a letter for you from Fern in my bag. I'll get it for you later.'

Charlie glanced over his shoulder. 'The corn smells like it's ready, so how do you feel about some flaked crab *au gratin* to go with it?'

'You can do all that up here?'

He crammed a chef's toque onto his head, tilting it at a rakish angle. 'My corn will have your taste buds crying for mercy.'

'No wonder I was dropped.' Louise stood up carefully, steadying her pod chair as it continued to rock to and fro. '*My* efforts had everyone crying for me to stop.' She peered over Charlie's shoulder as he unwrapped the foil from the corn and drizzled hot garlic butter over it.

'You can sort out the table,' he said, waving a cooking fork at her, 'while I give the corn a final turn.'

The sun began to disappear from the day, turning the skyline deep scarlet.

Charlie lit tea lights and placed them strategically around the decking. 'Romance on a shoestring.' He grinned.

'Exactly how many romantic evenings have you had up here?' Louise felt emboldened to ask.

'If you look behind the barbecue, you'll see hidden away a widescreen television. I get the boys up here and we watch football, phone up for a takeaway and behave badly — you know, male stuff.'

'And Pia?'

Charlie paused. 'She doesn't come up here anymore.'

Louise had the feeling she was trespassing, and that to ask more questions would be prying.

Charlie placed two art deco patterned plates on the wooden dining table. 'I cooked the new potatoes earlier and kept them warm in a stone oven. The mint was freshly picked an hour ago. Tuck in.'

Louise forked up some of the crab.

'What do you think?'

She closed her eyes, savouring every

mouthful. 'I've never eaten anything like it in my life,' she admitted.

'I hope that's a compliment.'

'It is.'

Charlie's look of anxiety was replaced by a smile as Louise forked up more crab flakes. 'I've got rhubarb *mille-feuille* for dessert, then some gingerbread-dust *petits fours* to follow. It's the revised menu I was going to serve to Quentin Voisin.'

'His loss, our gain,' Louise said, adding, 'Sorry. I know it's rude to speak with your mouth full.'

'Carry on. We're not standing on ceremony tonight.'

Louise stopped in the middle of mopping up the last of her crab with some crusty French bread.

'What's the matter?'

'I can hear a wasp.' She looked round nervously. 'It's getting louder.'

'It's not a wasp.' Charlie retrieved his mobile from behind a tub of azaleas. 'It's my new ring tone. Fern set it up. Let it go to voice mail.'

'What if it's an emergency? Who's looking after the girls?'

'Mrs Tolley's sleeping over; but you're right, I should answer it. Hello? Yes, she's here. Hold on.' He turned back to Louise. 'My daughter wants a word with you.' He said into the phone, 'Don't be long; we're in the middle of dinner.'

'Louise?' an excited voice greeted her. 'I've got lots to tell you. I've put fresh flowers in your room, and Mrs Tolley has made you a lovely stuffed frog. He's big and green and wearing a golden crown.' Fern giggled. 'Mrs Tolley says you have to kiss lots of frogs before you find your prince. He's on your bed and I can't wait to show him to you. When are you coming back?'

'Nothing's actually been arranged,' insisted Louise, glancing at Charlie, who was busy attacking his corn.

'Did you get my picture?'

'Drawing?' Louise mimed to Charlie.

'Sorry, forgot.' He flapped his hand, dropped his corn and began delving in his bag. In moments he held up a crude picture of a man with a skinny body, a huge head and lots of hair encased in a spotted bandana.

'Who is it?' Louise hissed back at Charlie.

'Not sure, but I think that thing in his hand is a musical instrument.'

'Could it be Rocko?'

Charlie broke into a grin. 'Now you mention it, I can see a resemblance.'

'When are you going to teach us to play the drums, Louise?' came Fern's voice.

'I'll have to get back to you on that one,' Louise said, evading a direct answer.

'Okay,' Fern agreed. 'I'll tell Gemma it's all arranged.'

'Hold on, Fern,' Louise cautioned, anxious not to make promises she couldn't keep.

'See you soon,' the child trilled.

'Forgot to tell you,' Charlie said as his daughter cut the call, 'Rocko wants to know where you are.'

'He knows where I went,' Louise replied. 'The old rascal told me he had no idea. He was rather rude when I told him what had happened. He suggested the situation was nothing less than I deserved.'

'That's his way of protecting me.' Louise smiled. 'I didn't physically contact him, but he knew I'd go home to my parents.'

When Louise had earlier waved goodbye to her mother and father, she had no idea where her life was going. And she still didn't, but she had known all along that she couldn't stay at home indefinitely. Her father relied heavily on her mother for everything, and Peggy didn't need any more stress in her life. After a good night's rest, her father was ready to go again, and Louise knew it was time to move on.

'Dessert?' Charlie asked. 'If you've got room.'

'I've always got room for dessert,' Louise replied, having finished every morsel of her crab with the help of the last piece of bread.

'There's cheese too, if you can

manage it with home-made quince jelly.' He loaded up the small table in front of them.

The tea lights cast lengthening shadows across the table as the sun finally disappeared behind the horizon. Louise swallowed the last cube of cheese. Her eyelids began to droop and she stifled a yawn behind the back of her hand. 'Sorry,' she apologised.

'I think that might've been the effect I was beginning to have on my viewers,' Charlie said, leaning back in his seat.

'You had an army of fans who cast me as enemy number one.'

'I felt bad about that. What happened wasn't your fault. The bosses didn't mince their words when they told me they weren't renewing my contract. Viewing figures were falling before you took over. You were the scapegoat. You didn't know?' He looked surprised.

'No one told me,' Louise admitted, feeling a weight shift from her shoulders.

'It was inevitable, I suppose. The

format needed updating. They made the right decision to pull the programme. They needed to attract a younger generation. Stories about me and my granddad didn't do it for them.'

'At the time you were pretty mad with me,' Louise said, recalling his reaction to her appointment as his replacement.

'I apologise. My chef's temperament has to have an outlet, and you were the target. But now maybe you can understand why I wanted out. I was turning into the sort of person I don't like. Can we draw a line under the past and get on with the future?'

'Mine or yours?'

'Ours. What do you think of renaming the restaurant the Dover Soul, spelled S-O-U-L? Grandpa Irons really did live there. Do you like the idea?'

'I think so.'

'Those stories I used to tell about him on air were my way of honouring his memory. He was the most marvellous man I knew. After my mother died, it was just him and me. We faced the world together and we managed pretty well.'

'He'd be proud of you.'

'I hope so.' Charlie gave a self-conscious smile. 'Back to business. It's early June now.' He looked thoughtful. 'Perhaps we might be ready to open by the end of July?'

'That soon?'

'We can't afford to delay. The public are fickle. If you're not in the news, they soon forget you. I've been having some ideas about you and me.'

Suddenly Louise didn't feel so sleepy anymore.

'We could play up the angle that we're now working together. You know, two old foes join together to overcome adversity? What do you think?'

'It might work,' Louise acknowledged, 'if I agree to come back.'

'We all miss you.'

'It's only been a day.'

'The workmen won't drink my tea. They say it tastes funny.'

'And Gemma?'

'It'd be wrong of me to promise an easy ride, but if she has a constant presence in her life she might settle.'

'By constant presence, you mean me?'

'Yes.'

'Have you discussed things with Pia?'

'She'll come round to the idea in time. Pia likes the glamorous life. She's not the sort to stay in one place for long, and she's got the sense to realise it's a good solution.'

'We have to trust each other, otherwise there's no point in going on.' Louise could feel the last of her resistance crumbling.

'Agreed. I'm totally up for it. Are you?'

The adjacent rooftops were now a sea of twinkling lights, and she could hear the murmur of voices as Charlie's neighbours made the most of the evening air.

'Would you like to sleep on it?' Charlie suggested. 'You can choose whichever room you like. There's only a choice of two. The sleeping bags are in the hall, and you'll find everything you need in the bathroom.'

'Which room do you prefer?'

'It's such a lovely night, I might sleep al fresco under the stars.' He moved in closer. Louise's cheeks began to glow.

'In that case, it's been a long day. Thank you for dinner.' She made to turn away but got no further. Charlie drew her into his arms and kissed her.

'There.' His voice was a soft murmur. 'Now we're friends again.'

Louise stepped back and narrowly missed stumbling over a flowerpot. 'Good night,' she mumbled, her head in a whirl. 'I'll see you in the morning.'

8

Louise blinked into the sunshine. Someone had strung red, white and blue bunting across the arch over the gate at the top of the drive leading down to Brooks Farm. It flapped gaily in the late morning breeze.

The journey from Charlie's flat back to the farm had taken longer than usual due to their late start and the density of the traffic. Louise had tailed Charlie's powerful Italian car, often losing sight of him as he roared off into the distance every time there was a straight stretch of road.

Charlie ambled towards her after he had unlatched the barred gate and leant against her driver's door. 'Looks like you're expected,' he said.

Louise wound down the window. 'How do you know the bunting's for me?'

'They don't normally hang out the flags on my account. I'm too much of a grumpy old so-and-so to get that sort of treatment.' He straightened up. 'The smart money says the reception's in your honour.'

'How did anyone know I was coming back?' Louise subjected him to a steely glare.

A look of guilt spread across Charlie's face. 'It was me,' he admitted. 'I let slip the news to Mrs Tolley. What was I supposed to do? She answered the telephone when I rang to check on the girls.'

'You could've been discreet.'

'I don't understand big words.' He grinned.

'‘Discreet’ isn't a big word.'

'Remember, you're talking to a boy who preferred to go fishing with his grandfather rather than attend school.'

Louise had difficulty believing the image Charlie painted of himself. He was as shrewd as they came. 'What are we going to do?' she said.

'Face the music? You'd best drive down first.'

'Why?'

'I'm not exactly flavour of the month. Everyone blamed me when you walked out.'

'I wonder why.'

'I thought it was a bit mean too,' Charlie agreed. 'Are you ready for the fray?'

Louise raised her eyebrows; then, taking a deep breath, she turned her steering wheel hard right. Charlie stepped back and waved her through. As she glanced back through her rear-view mirror, she saw him talking earnestly into his mobile phone.

Louise bumped down the rough road leading to the farmhouse. With her window still open, she detected singing. As she turned into the main drive, her foot faltered on the accelerator, then slipped off the pedal, stalling the engine.

Standing on the front doorstep was Mrs Tolley, her husband, about half a dozen workmen grinning from ear to ear, a petulant Gemma slouching against a doorpost, and Fern holding up a cake decorated with what looked like a million candles. The source of the singing was Rocko belting out a protest anthem on his famous guitar. Everyone appeared to be joining in with gusto, inventing their own words and having the time of their lives.

Rocko finished on a high note, then downed his guitar. 'At last. Come here.' His embrace left Louise struggling for breath. The fringed tassels of his leather jacket tickled her nose. He kissed her forehead. 'Is everything cool?' he murmured into her ear. 'Because if it's not, give me the word and I'll have you out of here in seconds.'

'Do you think you could ease up a bit? I can't breathe.' Louise found it difficult to move her lips. 'And I'm still standing,' she added, using one of their pet phrases.

Rocko patted her shoulder and released his hold. 'Just checking base.' He picked up his guitar and began strumming a few chords.

'Did you have to welcome me with a protest anthem?' Louise straightened her T-shirt.

'It was the only song we all knew.' He raised a clenched fist and everyone cheered again. 'Any more requests?' he asked.

'Louise,' Fern said, hopping up and down with impatience. The candle flames fluttered alarmingly.

Mrs Tolley placed a restraining hand on her arm. 'Steady, dear. We don't want any accidents.'

'Look what we've made you. It's a welcome-home cake. I helped Mrs Tolley ice it.'

'And we're parched for a cuppa,' one of the workmen put in, 'so when you're ready it's milk and two sugars all round.'

'Was this your doing?' Louise turned on Charlie, who had now caught up with her.

'I had nothing to do with the cake — that was Mrs Tolley — but I was in on everything else.'

'Speech,' someone called out.

The cry was taken up. Blushing furiously, Louise tried to protest as she was manhandled onto an upturned bucket. The little group looked expectantly in her direction.

'Thank you,' she said, struggling to find the right words. 'I'm overwhelmed. I don't know what else to say.'

'Then keep it short,' Rocko called over. 'Best to leave them wanting more.'

Mrs Tolley clapped her hands. 'Right, everyone — into the kitchen. Louise, when you cut the cake you must make a wish.'

Rocko gave a throaty laugh. Louise glared at him. She could read him like a book, and at times he could be infuriating. 'Before you start spreading rumours,' she said, hoping her voice was low enough for no one else to overhear, 'there's nothing going on between Charlie and me.'

'Did I say there was?' he asked, his eyes suspiciously innocent.

'You didn't have to.'

'Lovely sunset last night. Did you see it?'

Louise's blush deepened. 'I said leave it.'

'Have it your own way. But if the situation develops into a meaningful relationship, I want to be the first to know.'

'It won't,' Louise assured him.

'Come on, you two,' Arthur Tolley called over. 'You're missing all the fun.'

'Be right with you.' Rocko linked arms with Louise. 'How's my dear brother?' he asked.

'He had a fall.'

'Up at that allotment of his, I suppose.'

'Luckily it was nothing serious.'

'Perhaps I'll visit. It's been a while since I've seen the old boy.'

'What are you whispering about?' Charlie asked.

'Family stuff,' Rocko replied.

'Time to cut the cake,' Mrs Tolley said, beginning to grow impatient.

Rocko waved in her direction. 'Lead on, Alice — I'm starving.'

'You're always hungry, Rocko. I don't know how you stay so thin.'

'It's my healthy lifestyle.' He laughed.

They shuffled forward. Gemma, her arms crossed and still wearing her uniform leggings over a large T-shirt and fedora, glared at everyone in sulky silence.

'Hello, Gemma,' Louise greeted her. 'I hear you want to learn to play the drums.'

'Maybe.' Gemma shrugged.

'It's only a deal if you're polite to my Louise,' Rocko insisted. 'Any trouble and the deal's off.'

A guarded look came into Gemma's troubled dark brown eyes. Her shoulders slumped. Louise took pity on the girl. She could see so much of her teenage self in her sullen behaviour. 'Then we'll have to see that doesn't happen, won't we? Now why don't you help Fern with the cake before she drops it?'

The kitchen was a hubbub of noise, chaos and confusion, with everyone trying to help.

'You don't want to reconsider?' Charlie

murmured in Louise's ear as plates of cake were passed round together with mugs of hot tea.

Louise felt a lump rise in her throat. Even before his accident, her father had suffered from nervous anxiety, and family life had occasionally been fraught. Rocko had been her only refuge when things got the better of her father. The scene in front of her was exactly how she imagined a family life should be — warm and comforting, with the occasional squabble, but always welcoming.

A slice of cake on a plate was thrust into her hands. 'Are you going to eat all that?' Charlie's eyes widened.

Louise picked up a fork. 'I didn't get any breakfast, remember?'

'Only because you overslept.'

'Only because you didn't wake me.'

'What's with the huddle in the corner?' Rocko called over.

'State secrets,' Charlie called back.

'Leave them alone,' Mrs Tolley berated him, 'and make yourself useful, young man, by boiling up the kettle. We need more hot water.'

'You can have a waterfall of hot water if you call me a young man, my darling Alice.'

'I had no idea Mrs Tolley's first name was Alice.' Charlie looked on in wonderment.

'No one is immune to Rocko's charm.' Louise began forking up her cake.

'What's his real name?' Charlie asked, following her example. 'I mean, it can't be Rocko, can it?'

'Now that really is a state secret.'

Rocko, who had overheard the exchange, sauntered over. 'Only to be revealed on pain of death,' he said. 'Are we hanging out tonight, Louise? Could be a late one.'

'Your late ones always turn into early mornings, Rocko.'

'Do you have a problem with that?'

'I do tonight.'

'I don't know what's wrong with the younger generation,' Rocko grumbled. 'When I was your age, every night was a late one.'

'Some of us have to work for our living,' Charlie reminded him.

'*I* work,' Rocko protested.

'I'm talking proper work,' Charlie retaliated.

'I don't call cooking a salad work.'

'Stop it, you two,' Louise interrupted. 'Rocko, thanks for the invite, but another time?'

'Party poopers,' Rocko mumbled. 'The young today have no stamina. I suppose you're not interested in an all-night gig, Alice? With Arthur of course,' he added, catching the look on Mr Tolley's face.

'Another time, perhaps.' Flustered, Alice flushed. 'Now where's that hot water?'

'Coming right up.'

* * *

Charlie was ready to go early the next morning. 'Fact-finding mission,' he informed Louise. 'Any emergencies, you can reach me on this number.'

'What's on the agenda today?' she asked.

'Keep an eye on the workmen; look

after the girls; take messages; liase with Mrs Tolley; Marc the interior designer may drop by later. He's got a few ideas regarding décor.'

'So soon?'

'Things are coming along. Come on Fern, Gemma,' Charlie bellowed. 'I haven't got all day.'

Footsteps pounded the stairs, and Fern, her plaits flying out behind her, ran into the kitchen. 'Where's my bag?' she said.

'Here.' Louise held it up. 'Have you got everything?'

'My project,' Fern gasped, and promptly disappeared.

'Just as well I said I'd take them to school this morning,' Charlie remarked. 'They've probably missed the bus now anyway.'

'If you're pushed for time, I can take them,' Louise volunteered.

Charlie lowered his voice as if he didn't want to risk being overheard. 'I have to get the things Gemma lifted back to Mrs Young.'

'What's she going to do with them?'

'We agreed that Gemma would write letters of apology to all concerned, then she and one of the teachers are going to return them to their rightful owners.'

Gemma slouched into the kitchen. She was wearing regulation school uniform of grey pleated skirt and white blouse. Her hair was tied back in a neat ponytail. She looked like the perfect schoolgirl save for the sulky expression on her face.

Fern was soon back, waving a sheet of paper under Louise's nose. 'Will you help me with my project? You know all about the environment, don't you?'

'If I get a spare moment, we'll look at it together.' Louise hugged her. 'Now off you go and have a good day.'

'Come on, Gemma.' Fern picked up her bag.

Gemma hung back, reminding Louise of a cornered animal — one false move and she might lash out. Louise held out her arms and felt the young body stiffen as she hugged her. 'I'm very proud of you too, Gemma,' she said.

'What for?' The girl pushed Louise away.

'Having the courage to say sorry. It's not easy, and not many people can do it.'

'I didn't want to.' She looked down at the floor. 'And I don't see why I should.'

'Then you've learned an important lesson in life. We all have to do things we don't want to.'

'I hate wearing this uniform, and I hate you.' She snatched her bag off the table, and without a backward glance scuffed her way outside.

The farmhouse was quiet after everyone had departed. Louise poured herself a coffee and sipped it quietly, relishing the silence before the first of the workmen arrived for the day. She realised Gemma would need delicate handling if she weren't going to go off the rails again. She glanced at the sheet of paper Fern had thrust at her. It was entitled 'How I Can Protect the Environment'.

The builders' foreman poked his

head through the kitchen door. 'Morning. Just to let you know, we're here for the day. Good party yesterday.'

Mrs Tolley was hot on his tail. 'Glad to see things are getting back to normal.' She donned her apron. 'Where would you like me to start?'

'You don't need me to tell you that, Mrs Tolley.' Louise rinsed her coffee mug under the tap.

'As you wish. Mr Irons always gives me a free hand, so I'll carry on as usual, shall I?' Humming to herself, she began sorting out her cleaning equipment. 'I nearly forgot.' She delved into her carrier bag and produced a magazine. 'Did you see this?' She pointed to an article on the features page. 'Quentin Voisin has published a comment in the social column.'

'Down in deepest Sussex,' Louise read, 'lurks a cowshed that I am reliably informed will be the place to eat. Watch this space.'

'Is he the one who looks like a ferret in a bow tie?'

Louise hid a smile. Mrs Tolley's description of the food critic was spot on. 'That's the one.'

Mrs Tolley sniffed. 'I suppose he's referring to us?'

'I suppose he is,' Louise agreed.

'Well we don't want his sort here anyway, unsettling everybody.'

'I'll be over in the office if you need me, Mrs Tolley.'

The older woman went rather pink in the face and looked positively girlish. 'Thank you, dear. And it's Alice; no need to be so formal.'

'Thank you, Alice,' Louise said.

'Your uncle Rocko's quite a one, isn't he? Makes a girl feel young again. Arthur thought he was outrageous. I mean, your uncle virtually asked me out on a date. Not that I would have accepted, of course,' she finished on a regretful sigh.

Hiding a smile at the idea of Rocko and Alice going out on a date, Louise traipsed across the forecourt and climbed the wooden steps to the office. Rocko's teenage sweetheart, Emerald

DeVine, a rhythm and blues icon whom he'd married on her eighteenth birthday, had been the love of his life.

'No one could ever replace her,' he'd told Louise at Emerald's memorial service, where everyone had been asked to wear white and carry a red rose. The sound of Rocko's croaky voice singing one of his protest anthems to the accompaniment of the cathedral organ had been the most moving experience of Louise's life, and she hadn't been the only one wiping away the tears as he bowed his head at the end of his tribute.

Louise was forced to shoulder open the jammed door to the office. She gazed in despair at the mountains of paperwork. Then, with a weary sigh, she sat down and began to plough through the backlog. It wasn't until a movement behind her caught her attention that she remembered Charlie had told her to expect a visitor. She looked up, but it wasn't Marc Greenwood standing in the doorway.

'Sorry to interrupt,' a smartly dressed

woman said with a smile. 'The house-keeper said I'd find you here.'

'Can I help you?' Louise asked.

'You're Miss Drew?'

'Yes.'

'I'm Saffron Weekes.' She paused expectantly.

'If you have an appointment with Mr Irons, I'm afraid he's not here.'

'I do and I don't,' Saffron Weekes replied with a disarming smile.

Louise massaged the back of her neck. 'You're going to have to run that past me again.'

'Do you mind if I take the weight off my feet?' Without waiting for Louise's assent, she settled herself down in a rickety leather chair that had appeared from somewhere. 'My card.'

Louise inspected the businesslike logo. There was a thumbnail photo of Saffron in the corner. 'You've an impressive list of qualifications,' she said.

'But you don't recognise any of them?' Saffron raised a well-plucked eyebrow.

'Are you in the catering business? If

you are, I have to tell you Mr Irons won't be recruiting for a while yet; but if you'd like to leave me your details I'll put them on file.'

'I'm a media research assistant.' Saffron's eyes narrowed. 'Don't I recognise you from somewhere?'

Louise always dreaded moments like these. 'I don't know,' she countered, 'do you?'

'Have we met before?'

'I don't think so.'

Saffron shook her head. 'No matter, it'll come to me.' She smiled. 'Now, let's get down to business.'

9

Saffron flicked back her tawny shoulder-length hair. She was wearing a casual pale blue V-necked top and navy-blue trousers, and was every inch the confident media professional. In the course of her career Louise had met many such graduates, all supremely ambitious and focused.

'Have you heard of Sub-Plots?' Saffron began.

'Is it a writing academy?' Louise hazarded a guess.

'No.' Saffron's smile revealed her perfect teeth. 'Although I agree it sounds like one. I think we're going to have to rethink our brand name, don't you?'

Louise gave a polite smile.

'We search out the unusual,' Saffron continued. 'It's a fascinating job.'

'I'm sure it is,' Louise agreed with a puzzled frown.

'And you want to know what I'm doing here?'

'Perhaps if you make an appointment when Mr Irons is here?' Louise eyed up her growing pile of paperwork.

'Not necessary. I'll come straight to the point. Mr Irons — Charlie — might be interested in our services.'

Louise's suspicions were aroused. 'Are you a reporter?'

'No, I'm not,' Saffron was quick to reassure her.

'Then why is Sub-Plots interested in Mr Irons?'

'He'd make an excellent subject.'

'In what way?'

'We're only at the drawing board stage, you understand.' Louise waited for Saffron to go on. 'We're putting together a series of pilots, a portfolio of potential submissions to various producers. We're hoping to generate interest in an exciting new project.'

'Are you saying you're thinking of making a television programme on Charlie?'

'I've approached several other parties

who've expressed their interest in the project.'

'I'd like a direct answer, please,' Louise said, growing tired of Saffron's corporate speak, which she was finding difficult to follow.

'If I could persuade Charlie Irons to take part, with his significant media profile and faithful fan base, I'm certain we could have a hit on our hands. He could be the deal breaker.'

'Whoa,' Louise cautioned, finally getting Saffron's drift, 'you're going too fast.'

'Sorry.' Saffron's charm bracelet jangled as she flicked back her hair, revealing huge hoop earrings. 'I always get carried away when I'm excited by a project.'

'Which you still haven't fully explained,' Louise reminded her.

'The bottom line is, if Charlie Irons would give us free rein to delve into his historical background, we're prepared to help finance his restaurant.'

'You want to dish the dirt on Charlie and make money out of it?' Louise was aghast at the idea.

'The offer comes without strings.'

'Nothing comes without strings,' Louise was quick to point out. 'You're in the business of making money, and you want to make money out of Charlie.'

'We're prepared to make a very generous offer.'

'You're also asking Charlie to make a big sacrifice.'

'Can he afford to turn it down?'

'What do you mean?'

'I'm not in the business of stirring things up, but ... Quentin Voisin?' Saffron gave a knowing smile.

'What about him?'

'You weren't exactly up to speed that day, were you?'

'How did you hear about that?'

'There are no secrets in this business, but I'm sure you get my drift.'

'I'm not sure I do.'

'Quentin Voisin is a powerful adversary. One bad word from him could mean restaurant ruin. You need to have him onside.'

'You can stop Quentin Voisin writing a bad review?'

'I wouldn't say we could fix it, but if he knew the identity of Charlie's backers, he might not be quite so keen to rubbish the Dover Soul — good name, by the way,' she said, oozing approval.

'Have you got something on Quentin?' Louise felt an unexpected pang of sympathy for the restaurant critic.

'Like everyone else, Quentin has his weak points, but there's no need to go into all that now. Charlie needs friends, good contacts, influential people who can help him. We're prepared to take on that role. I'm sure Charlie will see it that way. Aren't you?'

'It's too high a price to pay.'

'You think so?' Saffron arched an eyebrow.

'I know so.'

'I don't see it like that. He's a modern-day buccaneer. On that basis alone, he'd make an excellent subject. He's such a magnetic character, and everyone loves a rogue.'

Louise could feel her lip curling in distaste. 'There are no skeletons in

Charlie's life,' she insisted.

'No?'

Louise's head began to throb. She knew she was being outmanoeuvred by Saffron. She decided it was time she played her at her own game and found out exactly what she had in mind. 'Hasn't delving into family trees been done before?' she asked.

'Agreed. That's why we have to be different.'

'In what way?'

'The people we've nominated have something significant about them, something that would interest potential viewers.'

'What 'something significant' do you have about Charlie?'

Saffron leaned back and crossed one elegant leg over the other. Her smile now reminded Louise of a cat taunting a mouse. 'Those stories he used to tell about Grandpa Irons? They were a great source of entertainment, weren't they? His USP? Unique selling point,' she clarified when Louise frowned.

'Are you saying Charlie's grandfather is his USP?'

'Even if the audience wasn't interested in cooking, they'd tune in to hear Charlie's boyhood tales of life on a fishing boat. He'd hold them enthralled with his stories of how he skipped school, and how his grandfather taught him everything he knew, and what a good example he was to his young grandson.'

'Your point is?'

'Nothing is ever as idyllic as it seems.'

Louise was no longer able to keep her feelings under control. 'Is this some form of sophisticated blackmail?'

'Not at all.' Saffron brushed an imaginary speck of dust off her sleeve. 'Did you know that Charlie's grandfather was actually born Jacob Mason?'

'No.'

'Or that records show that the said Jacob Mason was adopted by Reuben and Eva Irons?'

'I don't think the fact Jacob was adopted is enough to whet a viewer's appetite.'

'There's more.'

'Whatever you have to say, I'm not in the business of listening. If you want to submit a proposal, put it in writing and I'll show it to Mr Irons. That's all I'm prepared to do.'

'I also found out,' Saffron went on, ignoring the interruption, 'that Jacob Mason was an evacuee. He was one of thousands of children who returned to London in the short space of six weeks at the end of the war.'

'Exactly, one of thousands,' Louise said. 'That doesn't make Jacob Mason or Charlie a special case. Now if you don't mind, I have to get on.'

Saffron held up a hand to indicate she hadn't finished. 'It's here that the story gets interesting. Despite strenuous efforts to reunite young Jacob with his birth parents, Stanley and Violet Mason, no trace of them could be found. They quite simply disappeared. Can you imagine the trauma this would cause?'

Despite her aversion to Saffron's proposal, Louise couldn't help being drawn into her narrative. 'Poor Jacob,' she said with genuine sympathy.

'See, even you're hooked.' Saffron smiled. 'Many people vanished about that time. There was so much confusion, and records weren't always accurately updated. It was a time of great upheaval. Jacob wasn't the only unclaimed child. It does tug at the heartstrings, doesn't it?' She used her clear blue eyes to full effect. 'A little boy on his own, not knowing what had happened to his family or what the future held.'

'What happened to Jacob?'

'He was placed in a reception area with the other children until it was decided what action to take.'

'I see.'

'I'd like to go further with this, but I need your help.'

Louise was jerked back to the present. 'As I've already explained, I can't get involved.'

'No pressure, of course.'

'My answer is still no.'

Saffron pursed her lips. 'I suppose

Charlie hasn't mentioned anything to you about his background?'

'We're hardly on those terms,' Louise admitted.

'What sort of terms are you on? How long have you known him?'

'On and off for about a year,' Louise hedged. It was important she tread carefully. It could only be a matter of time before someone as astute as Saffron Weekes would remember where she had seen Louise before.

'How did you meet?'

Louise longed to tell Saffron it was none of her business, but she dared not take the risk. Any adverse reaction would spike her interest. 'Through work,' she said.

'Hm.' Saffron now looked preoccupied, her attention elsewhere, as if she had lost interest. 'Why don't I leave you my folder of research? You'll find it fascinating reading. Old Jacob was quite a character in more ways than one.'

'I don't want it.'

Again Saffron ignored Louise. 'It

wouldn't do to let it get in the wrong hands, but I know I can trust you to take good care of it. Show it to Charlie.' She produced a second business card from her sleek black purse. 'My private number — I'm available twenty-four/ seven.'

Louise glanced at the card with distaste, sorely tempted to tear it up.

'When you have a window.' Saffron's smile didn't falter. Her confidence made Louise feel uneasy.

'As I've already said, you need to approach Mr Irons through the usual channels.'

'I've tried, but he doesn't have an agent.'

'He has a website.'

'I've tried that too. I've used all the media platforms he subscribes to but without success. Does he ever check his emails?'

'Not often,' Louise was forced to admit.

'I thought not. That's why I'm here today. I would've preferred to speak to him personally, but he's not exactly the easiest person in the world to get hold of, is he?' Saffron shrugged on her jacket and picked up her car keys. 'I nearly forgot,' she added as she turned back to face Louise, 'I did manage to get hold of Mrs Irons.'

'You've spoken to Pia?'

'I contacted her agent, and he indicated that Ms McDonald might be onside if we delivered an attractive package. She's out of the country at the moment, but as soon as she gets back he promised to have a word with her.' Saffron paused. 'So where are you on this one? Are you in or are you out? I can assure you of our absolute discretion.'

'I'm not the right person to approach,' Louise insisted.

'Nonsense. You're the perfect choice. I'll be in touch.' She tapped the folder still on Louise's desk. 'Happy reading.'

A faint smell of lily of the valley lingered in the room after Saffron swept out. Louise sat where she was for a few moments, feeling as though she had been flattened by a force-ten gale; then with a sigh she closed down her computer. The girls would be home soon and she needed to get back to the farmhouse.

As she prepared to lock up the office, she realised the key was missing.

10

'Hi, how are things going?' Charlie asked. He'd rung up that evening on the dot of seven.

'No new dramas,' Louise replied. 'How's everything with you?'

'The usual hassle.' He sounded tired. 'People are keen to discuss contracts and all that, but when it comes to talking money it always starts to get difficult.'

'You should employ an accountant.'

'I don't need one at this stage.'

'What about an agent?' Louise persisted, still sore from her interview with Saffron.

'Don't think I haven't tried, but getting one isn't easy.'

'While we're on the subject,' Louise continued, warming to her theme, 'you could also try checking emails occasionally or looking at your social media contacts.'

'What's this all about?' Charlie now sounded suspicious. 'Who have you been talking to?'

Louise opened her mouth to reply, but before she could speak Fern sped into the downstairs study, leaving the door wide open behind her. 'Is that Daddy? Let me talk to him.'

'In a minute.' Louise held the receiver away from Fern's anxious hands.

'Purlease,' she pleaded, hopping from one foot to the other. 'I have something huge to tell him. I was chosen for the school swimming team. Miss Bates said my times were the fastest she'd ever seen and that we're certain to win the cup. I have to talk to Daddy.' Her voice went up an octave.

Through the open door, Louise glimpsed a shadow sneaking down the corridor. 'Where's Gemma?' she asked.

'Don't know.' Fern gave an unconvincing shrug.

'Yes, you do.'

'I'll only tell you if you let me speak to Daddy,' she bargained with a shade of her old belligerency.

'Answer my question,' Louise insisted.

'She's going out,' Fern mumbled, looking down at the carpet.

'Who with?'

'The biker boys on the green.'

'Is that Fern's voice I can hear?' Charlie asked down the line. 'What's going on?'

Louise threw the receiver at Fern and leapt out of her seat.

'Daddy,' Fern squealed down the line, 'guess what?'

Louise accosted Gemma by the back door. She was dressed in glittery tights, a short skirt and a sparkly top. She had tied a bright red ribbon around the brim of her fedora, and her eyelashes were clogged with black mascara.

'Where are you going?' Louise demanded.

'Nowhere,' was the sullen reply.

'In that case you won't mind if I close the door, will you?'

'Hey,' Gemma protested, 'what did you do that for?'

'If you're not going anywhere, it doesn't need to be open, does it?'

'I wanted some fresh air.'

'The truth,' Louise insisted.

'I don't know what you mean.' Gemma picked at a loose sequin on her top.

'You know exactly what I mean. You weren't getting a breath of fresh air dressed like that.'

'So what if I wasn't?' Gemma challenged. 'This place is dead at night. There's nothing to do round here.'

'Where were you going?'

'Out with some friends.'

'What friends?'

'No one you know.'

Fern raced into the kitchen then stumbled to a halt. 'Daddy says goodbye and to tell you he'll call again tomorrow.'

'You told her.' Gemma glared at Fern.

The smile drained from Fern's face. 'I didn't say anything.'

Gemma cast a disgusted look in Louise's direction. 'Then how did she know I was going out?'

'I saw you in the hall when Fern left

the door open,' Louise cut in. 'Now what's this all about?'

'Thanks a bunch.' Gemma said to Fern, two bright red spots of anger staining her cheeks.

'What for?' Fern looked bewildered.

'I thought you were my friend.'

'I am.'

'Of course you can go out, Gemma,' Louise intervened, 'but not during the week. You've homework to do, and if you do want to go out then I have to know where you're going and who with.'

'I'm going up to my room, and I don't want to be disturbed,' Gemma replied. 'Does that satisfy you?'

'I'm coming with you,' Fern insisted.

Louise sank onto one of the kitchen chairs with a sigh and finished off the coffee she had been drinking when Charlie's call had come through. It was cold and gritty and the taste made her shudder. Dealing with a mixed-up teenager had to be one of the worst jobs she had ever undertaken. Louise desperately wanted to help Gemma, but no matter how hard she tried, she failed to bond with the girl. She also felt troubled about how easily Fern could fall under Gemma's influence.

Throwing the remains of her coffee down the sink, Louise made sure the back door was locked and pocketed the key. The action reminded her she would have to look for the misplaced office key tomorrow, but meanwhile she definitely did not want the back door key going astray. It was only later that Louise remembered in all the confusion that she hadn't mentioned Saffron Weekes to Charlie.

The next morning, Louise searched for information regarding the forgotten evacuees who returned to London at the end of the war. Several websites came up. It wasn't difficult to discover that everything Saffron had told Louise was true. Newspaper reports showed that some children had been placed in holding centres. Despite intensive searches, no trace of their parents could be found. She presumed Jacob, Charlie's grandfather, was one of their number.

Louise bit her lip, reluctant to pry further into Jacob's past. Whatever had happened did not concern her.

The desk telephone rang. 'Is that my favourite niece?' Louise heard when she picked it up. She smiled at the sound of Rocko's husky voice.

'Hello, Uncle Rockford,' she teased him.

'I've told you never to call me that.' Louise could almost hear him cringe. 'Why your grandparents landed me with that name, I'll never know.'

'The eldest male in the family is always called Rockford — family tradition.'

'Man, that sort of thing went out with tea on the lawn and crinolines.'

'I expect you remember them well.' Louise laughed.

'You're lippy today. I've a good mind not to tell you why I called.'

'Why *did* you call?'

'Nancy Niceday is back in town.'

'That's terrific.' Louise broke into a smile of delight. 'When do I get to see her?'

'That's more like it,' Rocko approved.

Nancy and Rocko went back forever. Nancy Niceday and Emerald Devine, Rocko's wife, had been best friends. On stage together, the two girls were dynamite. Nancy's urban chic contrasted with Emerald's country girl appeal, and the fans loved them. Unlike Emerald, Nancy had never married. 'Wedlock would cramp my style,' she had insisted on more than one occasion. 'I'm a free spirit.'

She and Rocko maintained an easy relationship that suited them both. Neither of them was looking for commitment, but they were always happy in each other's company. Nancy travelled the world, singing at gigs whenever the mood took her. She detested routine and resolutely refused to tie herself to one band, preferring the variety of guesting with several groups, who all loved having her on board. Nancy Niceday's name on the bill ensured sell-out audiences.

'You can see her whenever you like,' Rocko said. 'She's staying over for a few days.

'Tonight?'

'Sure thing, if you can get it together. Just you, or are you bringing the gang?'

Louise thought back to the scene in the kitchen the previous evening. Perhaps this was the answer to her problem. 'Gemma and Fern have the day off tomorrow — it's teacher training — and we've promised them a session on the drums.'

'Then bring it on. How about treating Alice and Arthur to a night out too?'

'Rocko,' Louise chided, 'you'll be making Arthur jealous. Alice has taken a real shine to you.'

'Don't all the ladies?'

'One day you'll get yourself into trouble.' She laughed.

'That'll never happen. You're the only lady in my life. I'll arrange transport. What time do you need picking up?'

* * *

Nancy's flower-power van trundled into the courtyard as the light began to fade from the day. 'Hello, darlings,' she bellowed from the driver's window, hooting furiously. 'Are we ready to roll?'

Fern's blue eyes were wide with astonishment as the energetic redhead leapt out of the van and with arms outstretched enveloped Louise in a bear hug. The rainbow hues of her caftan fluttered in the dusk, giving her the appearance of an animated moth, and her bracelets jangled up her arm, revealing a vivid snake tattoo.

'You've got a snake,' Fern gasped.

'Do you like my transfer?' She held it out for Fern to inspect. 'I can make its scales dance.' She wriggled her fingers and the snake came to life.

'It's awesome.' Fern's voice was full of respect.

Nancy's bright green eyes glittered as they swept round the forecourt. 'Where's the other little lady?'

'Gemma didn't want to come, and I'm going to stay behind with her,' Fern announced, her face a picture of disappointment.

'You don't want to party?'

Fern's reply was an unconvincing, 'No.'

'I've never heard such a pack of lies in my life. Where's Gemma's room?'

'No, our room's private. You can't go in.' Fern tried to grab one of Nancy's sleeves but she wasn't quick enough.

'Hi, you must be Alice,' Nancy greeted Mrs Tolley, who had been hovering by the door. 'Are you and Arthur up for a night of high-octane fuel?'

Alice Tolley looked as if she wasn't sure what Nancy was talking about. She turned to her husband for support.

'We've volunteered to stay behind and look after the girls,' Arthur explained, 'to give Louise a night off.'

'Change of plan. Everybody in the van while I go and find Miss Gemma.'

'I really think I should go with you,' Louise insisted. 'You may need help.'

'Darling, when you've faced as many tough crowds as I have, a teenage girl with a touch of the moodys is not going to upset my mojo. Neither is she going to ruin everyone's evening.'

'What do you think?' Alice Tolley looked at her husband.

'Best do as she says,' Arthur replied after a moment's thought. 'She's right, you know — we all deserve some down time.'

'Now you're getting it, Arthur.' Nancy smiled approval.

She was back in less than five minutes, a reluctant Gemma trailing after her; and with everyone crammed into the back of the van, she turned the sound system up to full volume. 'This is the soundtrack of the Vegas gig I did last summer. Something to help you get into the mood.' She had to shout to raise her voice above the music.

Louise cast a sideways look at Gemma. Nancy appeared to have worked a miracle. Gemma was actually smiling now. Arthur and Alice were holding hands, and Fern was doing her best to sing along with the music. She sagged against her seat in relief. A dose of Nancy's special magic might be the medicine needed to clear the air.

Nancy swerved and narrowly avoided a car driving in through the gates. 'Whoops, who's that in the red roadster?'

'It's Daddy. He's home early,' Fern whooped.

'Party, Daddy!' Nancy bellowed, winding down her window. 'Rocko's pad. You've got half an hour to get there. Don't be late.'

'She's a card, isn't she?' Alice laughed as Charlie gaped at the violently patterned vehicle, his face a mixture of surprise and disbelief.

'She's more than that,' Louise replied, casting Nancy a loving smile. 'She's an experience.'

'Hold tight, gang,' Nancy said, putting her foot down on the accelerator, 'and prepare for the ride of your life.'

11

'You go and enjoy yourself, Louise,' Alice Tolley said. 'I'll keep an eye on Gemma and Fern.'

'What about our drum session?' Gemma had lapsed back into sulky mode. 'And where's Rocko?'

'Did someone mention my name?'

Fern whooped in delight as he ambled into their midst. 'Mummy's got a purple headscarf just like yours.'

'This is a bandana, if you don't mind,' Rocko corrected her with a mock frown. 'A present from the lovely Nancy.'

'I got the gang here, Rocks, all present and correct just like you said.'

'I don't see Charlie.' Rocko squinted into the darkness.

'He's following on behind,' Alice spoke up.

Rocko cast her a beaming smile that brought a flush to her cheeks. 'In that case, Louise can wait here for him while I personally escort the rest of you over to the VIP area.' He held out his arm and Alice linked hers through his. Before Arthur could protest over such familiarity, Nancy offered him her arm.

'I hope you'll be my escort, Arthur? I love a handsome man on my arm.'

His frown disappeared instantly. 'My pleasure,' he said.

'What's a VIP?' Fern whispered to Nancy, clinging onto her other arm.

'A very important person,' Nancy whispered back. 'So you and Gemma had better behave yourselves, otherwise Rocko may decide to demote you.'

'What does 'demote' mean?' Fern was still looking confused.

'It means you can't be one of his special people.'

'He wouldn't demote, us would he?' A worried look replaced the confusion on Fern's face.

'It has been known if someone misbehaves,' Nancy replied, looking hard at Gemma. 'Now are you ready to enjoy the evening?'

'S'pose so,' Gemma mumbled.

Nancy used her no-nonsense voice. 'Not good enough.'

'What do you want me to do?' Gemma pouted.

'Show some enthusiasm?' Nancy's natural exuberance shone through. 'Trust me, gang, we are going to have a great time. Are you on side with that, Gemma?'

'If you say so.' Gemma still looked unconvinced.

'There's Daddy!' Fern jumped up and down with excitement as Charlie drove into the compound. 'Is he going to join us on the drums too?'

'We'll see,' Louise murmured.

Catching the expression on Charlie's face, she wasn't exactly sure if he was in party mode.

'Leave the girls to me, LuLu,' Nancy insisted. 'I'll soon turn Gemma round. Give me five and she'll be eating out of my hand. Try to get Charlie to do the same — I mean, get him eating out of your hand, not mine. Talking of eating, he looks a mite hungry to me, and that's not good for the soul — Dover or otherwise.' She winked.

'I owe you one, Nancy,' Louise said.

'I'll make a note of it. Now enjoy. Alice, Arthur, girls, are we ready to party?'

Charlie, breathing heavily, strode towards Louise. 'What's going on?' He was dressed in jeans and a work-stained T-shirt.

'It's a gig,' Louise explained.

'I can see that, but what are we all doing here?'

'Rocko and I promised the girls a session on the drums, remember?'

'What are you thinking of? They have to go to school tomorrow.'

'No they don't. It's a teacher-training day. Come on, Charlie, chillax.'

Charlie opened his mouth as if to protest, then broke into a smile. 'Why not?' He shrugged on his black leather jacket. 'Do I look the part? It's been years since I've done this sort of thing.'

Louise's breath caught in her chest

with a stab so sharp she found it difficult to breathe.

'You okay?' Charlie frowned in concern.

Louise managed a shaky smile. She couldn't move. What on earth was wrong with her? She and Charlie didn't even like each other, yet at the moment all she could think about was his piercing blue eyes and how fantastic he looked in his leather jacket.

'Steady on,' Charlie called out as a noisy crowd shoved past them, causing Louise to lose her balance. With her hands flat on Charlie's chest, her heart began an uncontrollable thump against his ribcage. 'You're not about to faint on me are you?' His lips grazed her forehead. 'I don't think I'm up to carrying you back to the car.'

His words stung Louise into a reaction. Now was not the time to start wandering off into the realms of fantasy and wishing Charlie would kiss her again. 'I don't do fainting,' she said.

'Have you eaten anything today?'

'I had some breakfast — I think.'

'For goodness sake.' He grabbed her elbow. 'Come on.'

'Where are we going?'

'We're going to eat before we let it all hang out.'

'Nobody lets it all hang out these days.'

'Whatever. They certainly make a noise.'

'That noise is Rocko and the boys warming up.'

'My ears may never recover.'

'Rocko says playing his guitar on stage is like falling in love.'

'Spare me the details.' Charlie raised his eyes in a gesture of exasperation. 'And grab hold of this.' They were now standing by his car. He produced an old rug. 'Make yourself comfortable while I see to the supplies. We can sit in the boot.'

Louise settled down under the raised tailgate and dangled her legs over the exhaust as he produced a selection of plastic containers.

'There you go.' He sat down beside her. 'Want me to talk you through the menu, madam?' he asked as Louise peered into the various containers. 'For starters, we've got miniature stuffed vine leaves, chargrilled artichokes, black pitted olives, sun-dried tomatoes, and stuffed peppers. Is that enough to be going on with? Here, have some artisan bread.' He tore off a chunk and handed it over. 'See what you can do with that.' He passed over a paper plate and a serviette. 'It'll have to be finger food — I haven't got any forks — so tuck in.'

★ ★ ★

Louise finished off the last of the smoked salmon and leaned back with a sigh of contentment.

'I think we've found ourselves a new supplier, don't you?' Charlie did the same as they washed down their picnic with glasses of homemade fruit juice, which he explained had been given to him by another potential catering source.

161

'I thought you wanted to do all the catering.'

'A good chef knows when to out-source. I have my signature dishes, but everything else I leave to suppliers I can rely on. That way I don't get too stressed out.' He caught Louise's sardonic raised eyebrow. 'All right, I know I'm no great advert for keeping my cool, but all that is about to change.'

'You've had a makeover?'

The roar that went up from the warehouse drowned out Charlie's reply. 'Now what's happening?' He glanced over his shoulder.

'Nancy likes to make an entrance, and she knows how to whip up the atmosphere.'

'Who exactly is Nancy?'

'I suppose the best way to describe her is an old family friend.' Louise stretched out her legs.

'Would your old family friend mind if we gave her performance a miss?' Charlie wiped his hands on a moist tissue.

'We can't drive off,' Louise protested.

'I'm not suggesting we go that far, but I'm not sure I possess the stamina for a full-blown gig. I think the years are catching up on me.'

'What do we do if we don't join in with the music?'

'We could talk.'

'About what?'

'Us.'

Louise's heart began another triple beat.

'Why don't you tell me about yourself?' Charlie suggested. 'What's your signature dish?'

'I've got a weakness for chocolate biscuits crumbled over raspberry fool,' Louise admitted.

Charlie shuddered. 'That sounds seriously over the top.'

'Don't knock it if you've never tried it. Come on, it's your turn now. How did you get into cooking? Did you go to catering college?'

'I got my diploma, but I learned more about food and life in general being out on the water with my grandfather.'

'Was he a good cook?'

'I don't think he ever read a cookery book in his life.'

'There's something I've got to tell you,' Louise said.

'What?'

'We had a visit from a media research assistant called Saffron Weekes.'

'What did she want?'

'To look into your family tree.'

'Absolutely not.'

'She thought your grandfather would make a fascinating subject, and her backers are prepared to discuss terms with regard to the restaurant.'

'You mean in return for raking up my family history, they'll put money into my project?'

Louise wriggled uncomfortably against the metal strut of the boot mechanism. 'You can read up on her case notes if you like. She left me her card and a file of paperwork.'

'Then you can send it straight back to her.'

'Is her proposition such a bad idea?'

Louise asked. 'We both know the importance of publicity.'

Charlie looked into the distance before returning his attention to her. 'What I'm about to tell you must go no further.' She nodded. 'My grandfather was in trouble as a young man. You don't need to know the details, but he ended up in New Zealand, about as far away from this country as you can get.' He held up a hand before Louise could interrupt. 'He married out there. Then when his wife died, he came back home and moved into a seaside cottage in Dover. I suppose he thought if things turned nasty again, he could make a quick getaway.

'Anyway, Grandpa Irons bought a fishing boat and sold his daily catch to make a living. He worked hard. Whatever he'd done was in the past. When he wasn't busy he'd tell me all about the fish, and that's how I became interested in cooking. I don't want some busybody delving into his background and discovering all sorts of nonsense about him for the sake of publicity.'

A small shape shot out of the dark and collided with an inelegant bump against Charlie's legs. 'Found you.'

'Steady on.' Charlie put out a hand and scooped up his daughter.

'Rocko says if you don't come and see him perform, Louise is no longer his niece.' Fern wriggled in her father's arms. 'So I was sent to fetch you.'

'You shouldn't be running around the car park on your own in the dark,' Charlie chided her.

'Hello, there.' Alice Tolley flashed a torch in their direction. 'Fern's with me. Gemma's with Arthur having a session on the drums, and Rocko's ready to go on stage.'

'Come on.' Fern jumped down out of her father's hold and tugged his hand. 'We're missing all the action.'

Charlie made a half-hearted protest. 'Is there really no getting out of this?'

'Arthur says the atmosphere in there reminds him of our courting days,' Alice informed him.

Louise was forced to smother a smile

at the thought of the respectable Arthur Tolley chilling out with a bunch of rockers.

'In that case,' Charlie said as he closed the boot of his car, 'this sounds like something I shouldn't miss. Lead on.'

Fern and Alice were soon swallowed up in the darkness. Charlie draped an arm around Louise's shoulders. 'Watch your footing. I don't want you disappearing down a rabbit hole or being abducted by aliens, and tonight I have the feeling anything's possible.'

His body was warm and firm against Louise's. Her shoulder fitted comfortably against his chest as they picked their way across the muddy field towards the wall of noise.

* * *

'Have we really survived that experience?' Charlie asked as, arm in arm, they staggered out of the warehouse two hours later.

'Didn't you enjoy it?' Louise asked.

'Ask me when my hearing's returned to normal.' Charlie glanced at his watch. 'Have you seen the time? Where is everyone?'

'Nancy is rounding them up.'

'I hope she doesn't take too long. I would like to be home before dawn.'

Charlie turned on the ignition and eased his car forward as Nancy tooted past them, her flower-power bus swaying gently over the muddy ruts. Faces pressed up against the window waved back at them.

'How many people has she got on that thing?' Charlie asked.

'Not sure, but don't worry, she's a safe driver.' Louise rubbed her tired eyes as Charlie followed Nancy into the Brooks Farm forecourt. Parked in the centre was a car Louise did not recognise.

Charlie groaned.

'What's the matter?'

'That car belongs to Pia's agent, and if my eyes don't deceive me that's my ex-wife getting out of the passenger seat.'

12

Louise sat back with a worried frown. She had searched everywhere on her desk. Saffron's file was missing, along with her business card. She glanced at the empty hook on the wall. The misplaced key hadn't turned up either.

Charlie and Pia had taken the girls into town for a burger and to see a movie. Louise bit her lip. Was Fern up to her old tricks? Had she taken the file? Had Gemma dared her to do it?

The clock on the wall showed it was half past two. The family party wouldn't be back for ages. Louise knew she wouldn't be able to concentrate on anything until she had ascertained for certain that Fern didn't have the file.

She crossed the courtyard and entered the farmhouse through the kitchen door. 'I'm upstairs if anyone needs me,' she informed Alice Tolley, who was polishing the dining room table.

'Right you are,' Alice replied with her usual cheerful smile.

Glancing over her shoulder to make sure she wasn't being observed, Louise made her way upstairs; then, feeling like a criminal, she tiptoed along the landing. Although the two girls shared a room, Fern kept some personal things in her old room, and that was where Louise intended to start her search. She didn't like the idea of going through someone's private belongings, but necessity outweighed her conscience. She knew Saffron had discovered some very telling information about Jacob Mason, and Louise didn't want that information falling into the wrong hands.

Opening the wardrobe door, Louise crouched down and began rummaging around. There was nothing concealed amongst the coats and skirts or hidden under the winter boots and heavy shoes. She sat back on her heels to reassess the situation.

'What are you doing?'

Gemma's image was reflected in the wardrobe door mirror. Slowly straightening her legs, Louise stood up and brushed the dust off her leggings. 'I thought you were out,' she replied.

'I didn't go with the others.'

'Why not?'

'Because I didn't want to.' Gemma scowled. 'And you still haven't told me what you're doing here.'

'I was looking for something.'

'In Fern's room?'

'That's right. I've misplaced some paperwork.'

'Why should it be in here?'

'It isn't in the office, and the key is missing too.'

'And you suspect Fern?'

'I don't suspect anyone, but Fern did take the key once before, and I wondered if she'd borrowed it again.'

'So what if she has? It's her home, isn't it?'

Louise paused. 'Do you know anything about a missing file?' she asked Gemma.

The girl took a step backwards as if

she were scared to get too close to Louise. 'Why should I?'

'You and Fern do everything together. It wouldn't be the first time Fern's played a practical joke on me.'

'I don't know anything about any joke.'

'Gemma, it's important I get that file back, so if you have it can you give it to me and we'll say no more about it.'

Her request fell on deaf ears. 'I'm going to tell Charlie what you've been up to.'

Louise did her best to sound calm. 'It's your choice of course, but I don't think you should do that.'

'Why not? Don't you want him to know you're a thief?'

'I haven't stolen anything.'

'How do I know that?'

Louise made a gesture with her arms. She should have realised that searching Fern's room had been a bad idea. 'Why didn't you go to see the film with the others?' she asked, changing the subject.

'Because I was tired. Rocko kept us all up late, remember? I've only just got up.'

'Well now that you are up, do you have plans for the rest of the day?'

'I thought I might go out later.' Gemma affected a casual air as if she hadn't given the matter much thought.

'Where to?'

'I haven't made up my mind.'

'We could go out together if you like.'

'I prefer to go on my own.'

'That's not a good idea.'

'You can't stop me.'

'Louise?' Alice Tolley called up the stairs. 'I forgot to tell you Gemma didn't go out with the others. She's in her room.'

'That's okay, Alice. She's with me. I'll keep an eye on her.'

'Right-ho. I'm off now; I've got a dentist appointment.'

'See you tomorrow.' Louise waved out of Fern's bedroom window as Arthur drove into the forecourt to pick up his wife before turning back to Gemma. 'We could make a start on your project,' she suggested.

'What project?'

'The one Fern showed me, about the environment.'

Gemma smothered a yawn. 'Boring.' Her eyelashes looked suspiciously darker than usual, and Louise was convinced the girl was wearing a pair of Pia's earrings.

'I'll make a bargain with you, Gemma,' she said.

'What sort of bargain?' The wary look was back on her face.

'I won't tell Charlie or Pia that you planned to meet up with your friends on the green if you don't mention this little meeting.'

The astonishment on Gemma's face told Louise all she needed to know. 'I don't know what you're talking about.'

Louise pushed home her advantage. 'That's why you're wearing your new skirt and boots and my mascara, isn't it?'

'You can't prove a thing.' Two bright red spots of anger now stained Gemma's pale cheeks.

'But I'm right, aren't I?'

Gemma's eyes darted around the

room as if seeking inspiration. 'Who do you think Pia will believe, you or me, if I tell her I caught you in Fern's room going through her things?'

'I don't want to argue with you, Gemma,' Louise said, 'but I can't let you go out like that. It would be irresponsible of me.'

'You know why everyone's gone out today, don't you?'

'To have some quality family time together.'

'Pia thinks Charlie's got a thing going for you.'

Louise began to feel hot around the neck.

'They've gone out to get away from you.' Gemma's cheeks coloured up. 'And like you, I wasn't wanted.'

'That's not true.'

'Yes it is.' Gemma was now breathing heavily as she waited for Louise to react.

'Gemma.' Louise put out a hand to comfort her.

The girl took another step backwards. 'Don't touch me.'

'All right, I won't.'

'I hate it here.'

'Why?'

'You've no idea what it's like to be an outsider.'

'I know what it's like to be bullied at school.'

Gemma tossed back her head. 'No one bullies me,' she said with a show of bravado.

'That's good to hear.' Louise smiled. 'Why don't we go downstairs to the kitchen, and you can tell me what's bothering you?'

'You're only being nice to me because you're scared I'll tell Pia about you.'

'You've got it in one,' Louise agreed.

'You're not denying it?' Gemma's spiky eyelashes widened with surprise.

'Why should I? You're a smart girl. I can't fool you, can I?' Louise held her breath. Had her ploy worked?

'No one speaks to me at school except for Fern. I'm different from them. They've all been friends forever. They don't like me. I don't fit in.'

'You have to work at friendships,

Gemma. Give it time.'

'Some of the older girls meet up on the green. I heard them talking about it. One of them has a brother and they do all sorts of exciting things together. There are bikes and stuff.' She bit her lip as if fearing she had said too much.

'Gemma, you're too young to go out like that on your own.'

'I'm fourteen.'

'Not until next month.'

'If you don't let me go, I'll tell Pia you suspect Fern's a thief.'

'Then you'd better go ahead and tell her.'

'Where are you going?'

'Downstairs. I don't know about you, but I'm hungry.'

Gemma slumped against the bed.

'Would you like something to eat? Alice has baked some of her almond biscuits, and Charlie brought back loads of Mediterranean nibbles. Let's do a late brunch.'

'Could do, I suppose,' was the ungracious reply.

'And are you really sure you don't know where my file is?'

'I can't help it if you don't believe me, but it's the truth.'

'In that case, let's go downstairs.' Casting a last glance round Fern's old bedroom to make sure the wardrobe door was closed, Louise left the room.

Out on the landing Gemma mumbled, 'I'll be down in a minute.'

With the back door of the kitchen firmly closed, Louise checked that the front door was bolted, then set about making the preparations for their meal. After a quarter of an hour with no sign of Gemma, she opened the connecting door that led to the stairs.

'Where've you been?' she asked as a red-faced Gemma raced down.

'Looking for your file, but I couldn't find it,' she said in a rush.

Louise brushed aside what she suspected was an invented excuse. 'Never mind.' Gemma had probably been texting her new friends, but at least she hadn't sneaked out to join them on the green. 'Eggs?' She held up the omelette pan. 'To go with the mushrooms and Parmesan cheese?'

Gemma slid into the seat opposite and nibbled on some tomato bread, her eyes never leaving Louise. Louise turned back to the eggs.

'So, tell me about life in London before you came here.'

'What do you want to know?'

'Did you have lots of friends?'

'Some.'

'And what did you do on the weekends?'

'This and that.'

Louise flipped the sides of the omelette to the middle of the pan. Gemma appeared to have retreated back into sullen mode. 'Perhaps when things are more settled we can have a day in town. Would you like that?'

'If I'm still here.'

Louise turned round. Gemma was staring at the pine table, a small muscle tugging at the corner of her eye. 'Of course you'll still be here.'

'You don't know that. You don't know anything.'

Louise slid the omelette onto a plate, sliced it in half and served it up with some vine tomatoes, chopped chives and warmed artisan bread. 'There you are.'

'I'm not hungry.' Gemma pushed her plate away.

'You have to eat something,' Louise insisted.

'You can't keep me here a prisoner.'

'Whatever do you mean?'

'You've bolted the front door and I can't get out the back.'

'Gemma, what's wrong?' Louise asked in concern. 'Whatever it is, I'm sure we can sort it out.'

'No, you can't. No one can.'

'Is it school? You're not in more trouble, are you?'

The expression on the girl's face reminded Louise of a wounded animal. As if in sympathy, Millie meowed from the corner of the room. Louise placed a saucer of milk on the floor for her. When she looked up Gemma had gone.

13

'We need to think about a list of guests for the opening night.' Charlie was perched on a corner of Louise's desk. The sun slanted across his hair, turning it from its usual mid-brown to a warm chestnut colour. 'And we ought to consider a dress rehearsal. I'm playing with a few menu ideas and I'd like to give them a dry run.'

Louise looked up in surprise. 'So soon?'

'The workmen are on a bonus if they finish on time, and they've pulled out the stops. Marc Greenwood's got the décor sorted, and nearly everything else is in place. I'm keen to push things forward. We don't want to lose the moment. In this business you're only as good as your last *tarte tatin*. People soon forget a face. So, VIPs, CIPs — that's commercially important people to you.' He smiled.

'We need a brainstorming session. Any ideas?'

'Do you have anyone in mind?' Louise's head was too fuzzy to think straight. She was going to have to tell Charlie about the lost file, but there was never a right moment to approach the subject.

'I suppose we'd better have another go at getting Quentin Voisin onside.'

'Are you sure?'

'I know I said the man was yesterday, but he's an important contact.'

'You don't think he'll write a bad review because of what happened?'

'It's hard to tell. He's made mileage out of our little misunderstanding, so I think we'll have to put his name down.' Charlie scribbled a note on his pad, then looked up at Louise. 'Did you keep in touch with anyone from the old days?'

'No, did you?'

''Fraid not.'

They exchanged sympathetic smiles. Charlie's unruly hair had been tamed into tidiness and he was wearing a freshly ironed shirt and tailored chinos, not his usual work wear. Louise wondered briefly if the new dress code was Pia's influence.

'There must be some tame press guys who wouldn't mind a free meal.'

'Everyone likes a free meal,' Louise pointed out.

'In that case, make a list of anyone you can think of and we'll go through it together.'

'What about Rocko?'

'I wouldn't have thought the opening of a restaurant would be his sort of thing.'

'He knows a lot of people.'

'But he's not a foodie.'

'He'd be on our side.'

'What about that girl friend of his?'

'Nancy Niceday?'

'Is anyone seriously called Niceday?' Charlie's blue eyes twinkled with amusement.

Louise felt obliged to stand up for her old friend. 'It's her real name, and I think it's a terrific one. And she's a people person. She'll get things going. When she throws a party, you find count-esses dancing with refuse collectors.'

'She does have the knack of breaking the ice,' Charlie agreed, still smiling.

'And she worked wonders with Gemma.'

'Okay. Count her and Rocko in.'

'What about Pia?'

'You can never rely on models to be in the right place at the right time, and unfortunately a lot of them don't eat food — at least not the type of food I intend to serve. I want the guests to really enjoy what we give them, not push a lettuce leaf around the plate for an hour then insist they've eaten a huge meal.'

'Rocko's lot have healthy appetites.'

'He's not the only one in the family. I see you polished off the last of the Mediterranean samples.'

Mention of her solitary brunch reminded Louise of Gemma.

Charlie frowned at her. 'Anything wrong?'

'Nothing.' Louise feigned a yawn. 'I

haven't caught up with my sleep.'

'We're going to have to cut down on parties for a while. With only a few days left, dancing the night away is not an option.'

'Was Pia annoyed we kept the girls out so late?'

'What annoyed her most was missing all the fun. Fern was full of it in the burger bar.' Charlie swung his leg thoughtfully backwards and forwards. 'Talking of the girls, did Gemma open up to you yesterday?'

Louise chose her words carefully. 'Not really.'

'We tried to get her to come with us but she was in one of her moods, and there was no changing her mind.'

After Gemma had fled the kitchen, and with only Millie for company, Louise had devoured both halves of the omelette she had prepared, before finishing off the vine tomatoes and the stuffed peppers left over from the Mediterranean samples. Gemma had stayed in her room for the rest of the afternoon, and Louise, not wanting to leave her alone in the farmhouse, had done another search of the rooms to see if she could find Saffron's misplaced file, but without success. When Fern returned bursting with news about the film and the burger bar, Louise had seized the first opportunity she could to follow Gemma's example and retire to her room.

Pia had seemed disappointed when Louise turned down her offer of a scratch supper in front of the television, but Louise couldn't help remembering what Gemma had said about Pia's jealous nature. Treating herself to a long hot bath, Louise had clambered into bed and fallen instantly asleep.

'Pia thinks Gemma will settle and that we shouldn't make a fuss,' Charlie said. 'She says it's a phase all girls go through. The only person she really talks to is Fern, but I couldn't ask my daughter to betray a trust if Gemma told her things in confidence.'

'I think Gemma wanted to go out somewhere yesterday afternoon, but then she changed her mind and went to her room. That's all I can tell you.'

'She spends a lot of time in her room. I can't help feeling it's unhealthy. Let's hope Pia's right and that we're worrying unnecessarily.' Shaking his head, Charlie swung his legs off the desk. 'Best get on with the day. We'll have a walk around the site later when the workmen have gone, and you can see the progress they've made. It's coming together well.'

'Charlie?'

He paused next to the door.

'Those people who wanted to do the family tree thing?'

'What about them?'

'Have you read the file?' Louise asked.

'I haven't seen it.'

Any hope she had that Charlie knew of its whereabouts died.

'Have they been in touch again?' he asked.

'No.'

'Remember, if they do contact you, my answer is an emphatic no.'

'Even if they can provide finance and publicity?'

'Their sort of publicity I do not need; and as for finance, I'm off to see the bank manager now. Wish me luck.'

'Charlie,' Louise called out again.

'What now? I'm running late.'

'You haven't seen the office key, have you? You haven't borrowed it for any reason? I can't find it.'

'I expect it'll turn up somewhere. Must go. *Ciao*.' With a devastating smile, he clattered down the stairs. Through the open window Louise heard him talking to someone in the forecourt below. Moments later she heard footsteps on the stairs.

Pia pushed open the office door. 'Mind if I join you?'

'Of course not. Come in.' Louise did her best to sound enthusiastic. 'Take a seat.'

Pia crossed her legs in one elegant movement. Not a hair was out of place, and beside her Louise felt dowdy. Her shirt was stained with a green-coloured liquid, and apart from a touch of blusher and a slick of lipstick, she wasn't wearing makeup. Pia looked ready for the red carpet.

'I'd like to thank you for all you've done for my girls,' Pia began.

Louise was careful to keep her face expressionless.

'They're both at a challenging age, and it must have been difficult for you, not having children of your own.' Pia moistened her lips with the tip of her tongue. She reminded Louise of a tiger about to pounce. 'The thing is . . . ' She paused and adjusted the neck of her silk blouse. ' . . . yesterday was such a success that Charlie and I have talked things through and we've discussed the possibility of getting back together.' She looked expectantly at Louise.

'He hasn't mentioned anything to me,' Louise said, feeling as though she had swallowed a stone.

'It's early days.' Pia affected a light laugh. 'But we've realised the reason we broke up was no more than a storm in a teacup. Some silly girl had a crush on

Charlie and began behaving inappropriately. I mean, it's understandable.' The green-blue eyes narrowed. 'I'm sure you've noticed the effect he has on women.' She paused again. 'Anyway, when I realised what was going on, I totally overreacted. It was stupid of me. I see that now, but I want you to know how things stand between Charlie and me in case you got the wrong idea.'

'About what?' Louise picked up a stray pencil from the desk and rolled it between her thumb and forefinger.

'Charlie knows how to use his charm to get what he wants. It's important you don't misread any signals he may give out.'

'Our relationship is purely professional.'

'I'm not suggesting otherwise.' Pia looked amused. 'Charlie usually falls for the more sophisticated woman. But I thought I ought to have a word in your ear in case you might've been growing a tad too close to him for comfort. Rooftop dinners and al fresco picnics are all very well in their place, but you shouldn't read anything significant into them.' She arched an eyebrow. 'Don't look so surprised, Louise. Charlie tells me everything. I know all about what you and he got up to in the back of his car at that gig.'

The way Pia described the incident made Louise blush. 'It wasn't like that,' was all she could say.

'Charlie isn't an easy man to live with, believe me. He's temperamental, selfish, and totally focused on his career. And as I've already said, he's not above using people to get what he wants. I wouldn't want you to get hurt.'

'I understand.'

'I knew you'd be sensible about things.'

'When do you intend to move back to Brooks Farm?'

'We haven't decided on a date. Of course with Gemma now living with us on a permanent basis, there isn't an awful lot of space. Things are going to be rather cramped. I'd like to decorate

Fern's old room in case she chooses to move back into it. That of course means the only spare bedroom would be the one you occupy.' She waited for Louise to respond.

'Are you saying you want me to move out?'

'There's no need to do anything in a hurry, but give it some thought.' Pia uncrossed her legs and stood up, smoothing down her skirt. 'I'm so glad we've had this little talk. Don't feel you have to make a rushed decision, but I suggest you come to it sooner rather than later.'

There was a loud snap as Louise broke her pencil in half. It had taken Charlie's ex-wife to open her eyes. She had been in danger of falling in love with him. How it had happened, Louise didn't know. He was a family man, successful, charismatic, full of plans for the future — his future. In contrast, Louise was single with only a second-class degree in modern technology to her name. After her ignominious dismissal from the television studio, she had been unable to find work until Charlie had offered her a job. She owed him everything, and now she was going to have to start again.

'I'll leave you to answer your telephone.' Pia smiled and left the office.

In a daze Louise lifted the receiver. 'Brooks Farm.'

Saffron's breezy voice came down the line. 'Hi, how's it going? Have you had a chance to talk to Charlie Irons about our project?'

Louise did her best to rearrange her jumbled thoughts. 'He's adamant he doesn't want his family background being used as restaurant promotion.'

'That's a pity.' Saffron sounded genuinely disappointed.

Louise switched off. She wasn't really interested in anything Saffron had to say.

'Did you read my notes?' Saffron persisted.

'I thumbed through them.'

'Didn't you find the bit interesting about how his grandfather fled this country for New Zealand before the authorities could catch up with him?'

Louise took a deep breath. 'Saffron, Charlie's grandfather was his inspiration, and all you want to do is besmirch a fine man's memory for personal gain. So you'll have to forgive me if I don't share your enthusiasm for the project.'

'The last thing we'd want to do is upset anyone,' Saffron was swift to reassure Louise. 'We could play up the personal angle, you and Charlie.'

'There isn't one.'

'It came to me the other night while I was driving home. You're the woman who got Charlie Irons dismissed, aren't you? Now there has to be another story there, wouldn't you say?'

14

'Fern.' Louise was waiting for the child as she raced into the kitchen. She threw her schoolbag towards the windowsill, narrowly missing a snoozing Millie.

'What?' The girl made a dive for the biscuit tin.

'Have you been in the office recently?'

'Why?' She glanced towards Gemma, who was hovering in the doorway.

'You're not in any trouble, but I do need to know if you've seen the key or removed a file from my desk.'

'I don't go in there anymore,' trilled Fern. 'Daddy said I wasn't to. Besides, it's boring.' She wrinkled her nose. 'And it smells funny — paint and bricks and stuff.'

While Fern was speaking, Gemma streaked past Louise and disappeared up the stairs. 'Hey, wait for me!' Fern called. She scooped up a handful of biscuits before racing up.

Charlie ambled into the kitchen behind the girls and sat down at the table. 'What do you think of the menu?' He nodded to the lists Louise had been trying to study before Fern and Gemma arrived. As usual, the kitchen table was covered in paperwork. Charlie picked up the biscuit tin. 'That wretched thing gets everywhere.' He helped himself to a chocolate cream and put the tin on the dresser. 'Now where were we?'

Louise passed over a sheet of paper covered in his scrawled notes.

'Right, here we are.' He bit on his biscuit and munched thoughtfully as he ran his eyes down the suggestions he had made. 'I thought canapés first while the guests mill around, chat and get to know each other. They can have a good look at the premises while you pitch in with some sales talk — what do you say?' He peered at Louise over the top of his sheet of paper. 'Hello,' he prompted, 'input needed here.'

'Yes, very good,' Louise agreed hurriedly.

Charlie made a noise at the back of his throat. 'Hm. I think I'll serve up a good solid pot-roast chicken with masses of fresh vegetables, before finishing up with a choice of desserts — passionfruit sorbet, champagne jelly and chocolate soil. That should please the chocoholics. If anyone's got any room after all that, there'll be a selection of artisan cheeses and coffee with homemade *petits fours*.'

'I like a nice pot-roast chicken,' Alice Tolley said as she bustled through from the lounge. 'Is there going to be a dress code?'

'Wear whatever makes you comfortable, Alice.'

'That'll please Arthur. He's not one for suits.'

'Don't forget the vegetarians,' she said. 'My granddaughter is one. You did say she could come.'

'Tell her I'm making wood-mushroom pasta and a summer vegetable crumble. She can try a bit of both if she wants to.'

'She's been boasting to her school friends that she knows Charlie Irons, so if you're thinking about doing doggy bags she'll take the lot.'

'Once the builders get going I don't expect there'll be anything left, but I'll bear your suggestion in mind.'

'See you tomorrow, then,' Alice said with a cheerful smile.

'What if people don't like chicken and don't fancy the pasta?' Louise felt it was time she gave some input into the discussion.

'I'll poach a whole salmon in the kettle. Garnished and served cold, it should make an impressive centrepiece. Marc Greenwood is seeing to the drinks. His wife's got a friend in the business, and they can sort out glasses and all that goes with that side of things.' He looked expectantly at Louise.

'You've thought of everything.' She did her best to match her enthusiasm to that of Charlie's.

'Goodness knows how many deliveries we've got scheduled over the coming days. You'd better stock up on vitamin pills. We aren't going to get much time to eat.'

'That's not good advice from a celebrity chef.'

'I am not nor ever have been a celebrity chef. I'm someone who likes to cook.'

The expression on Charlie's face was one Louise had recognised many times before. This close to the big day, his temper would be running high. A careless remark would be enough to inflame a reaction. 'What else have you in mind?' She was careful to keep her voice steady.

'I'll do a running buffet,' a mollified Charlie suggested. 'That way I can cover most diets and allergies.'

'I don't think you've forgotten anything.' She hoped her smile was working properly; she wasn't sure she could keep up the pretence for much longer. She had lost an important file, and Charlie needed to know about it, though she dreaded to think what his reaction might be.

'That just leaves teas and coffees and light refreshments.'

'Charlie,' Louise cut in, but he wasn't listening.

'There's an urn about the place somewhere. We're going to have to set it up in here. Are you paying attention?' He was frowning at her again.

'Yes, of course. Teas. I'll speak to Alice.'

'You look distracted.'

'There's something on my mind.' She paused, preparing herself for fallout of monumental proportions.

'Nothing that can't wait, I'm sure.' Charlie's mood swings were mercurial and Louise was having difficulty keeping up with him. 'You know, I think the dress rehearsal is going to be more fun than the real thing. We'll have people there who really matter, those who've had a hand helping to create the Dover Soul — the workmen and their partners, suppliers, local tradesmen. We should get some genuine feedback. If they don't like anything, they'll let us know, that's for sure.'

Louise felt ashamed at the wave of relief that washed over her. There was no way she could break the bad news to

Charlie today. He wasn't in the mood to listen.

'I hope everyone likes the décor,' he said. In the end Charlie and Marc had opted for basic furnishings, lots of polished pine, bundles of herbs dangling from the wooden beams, and gleaming copper saucepans hanging on the walls. A south-facing paved terrace at the back afforded sweeping views across the open countryside, and Marc had gone for rustic furniture coupled with enormous garden umbrellas to shield those with more delicate skins from the sun or to act as shelter if it rained. Tubs of orange geraniums from the local garden centre added a vibrant splash of colour.

'Why wouldn't they like the décor?' Louise asked.

'Do you know anything about interior design?' Charlie flared up again.

Louise flinched. 'No,' she admitted in a hollow voice.

'Sorry.' Shamefaced, Charlie slid his hand across the table. 'You didn't deserve that. I always get like this before the big night — imagining the worst.'

Millie jumped onto the table with a loud meow. 'Come on,' Charlie said to Louise, 'shout back at me. I won't take offence.' Millie purred loudly as he massaged her ears. 'Friends?' he pleaded with an anxious frown. 'Millie puts up with me, don't you?' He received a whiskery nudge in reply as the cat rubbed her head against his chin.

'Perhaps Millie would like to take over my job,' Louise suggested.

'Would you?' Charlie tickled her under the chin. With a meow, the cat jumped off the table. 'Looks like the job's still yours.'

'Thanks,' Louise replied, wondering how much longer she would be in gainful employment.

'So, back to business. Acceptances? What's the situation there?'

'Lots of 'I'll be there if I can' replies.'

'And Quentin Voisin?'

'His assistant acknowledged receipt

of the invitation.'

'That's about the best we can hope for, I suppose. Quentin's far too important to commit. Right — you mentioned you had something on your mind?'

The sound of a van driving over the cobblestones distracted him. 'Fish man's arrived. I'd better see what he's got for the freezers and order a couple of fresh salmon. I need to give him plenty of warning; he can be a grumpy old so and so. Harry, how're things?' He greeted the dour fisherman with a beaming smile.

Louise made to follow him, but a movement in the doorway caught her attention. Gemma drew back to avoid being seen, but realising she was too late and that Louise had spotted her, said, 'I thought you were talking to the fish man.'

'Do you want something?' Louise noticed she was wearing the same outfit she had chosen on the day the family had visited the burger bar.

'I can be trusted, you know.'

It was then Louise noticed she was carrying a bag. 'What's in the backpack, Gemma?'

'Nothing.'

'I'd like to look inside.'

'That's an invasion of my privacy.'

Louise decided it was time to adopt a firm tone with the girl. 'Gemma, we can't go on like this. You have to tell me what's wrong.'

'Why should anything be wrong?'

'Is it school? Have you been into town again on your own? Charlie gives you an allowance. There's no need to take things.'

Gemma was still keeping a tight hold on her bag. 'I was going out for a walk, but I suppose you're going to stop me doing that.'

'We can go for a walk if you like. I have some free time.'

'I can go on my own. I'm not a child.'

'Where's Fern?' Louise asked.

'Doing her project. I offered to get some leaves to help her.'

'What sort of leaves?'

'Trees, you know. Environmental stuff.'

Louise sighed. 'Sit down, Gemma. There's something I have to ask you.'

'What?' Gemma slid into a chair, all the time looking down at the table.

'Did you remove the key from the office?'

She slumped. All the fight seemed to go out of her as with trembling fingers Gemma put a hand in her bag and withdrew the lost key from a side pocket.

'I found it,' she mumbled, adding in her defence, 'I didn't know what it was for.'

'Where did you find it?'

'I can't remember.'

Louise picked it up and decided not to pursue the matter. 'Never mind. Thank you for returning it to me.'

'Can I go now?'

'Not yet. I need to know about the file.'

'I don't know anything about a file. I knew I'd get the blame. I didn't take it.'

'I'm not saying you did, but it isn't

mine and I need to return it. This is really important.'

'Why don't you believe me?'

'Gemma, this isn't the first tall story you've told me, is it? I want to know I can trust you, and the only way I can do that is if you behave in a responsible manner.'

'Why should I? No one cares about me.'

'Yes, they do.'

'Anyway, you won't be here much longer, so it doesn't matter, does it? I heard Pia saying you've got to move out because it's too crowded in the farmhouse.'

'When did you hear her say that?'

'I was coming to find you to confess about the key, but when I heard her say there was no room for you I knew there'd be no room for me either, so I'm leaving.'

Louise felt the colour drain from her face. 'Gemma, darling, that simply isn't true.'

'It is. I heard her.'

'Charlie and Pia are your legal guardians.'

'But they're not my parents.'

'They are in all but name, and Charlie was so pleased when you came here to live. It made the unit into a proper family.'

Gemma raised a hopeful face towards Louise. 'You mean Fern, me, you and Charlie?'

'Something like that,' Louise gave a guarded reply.

'Then I won't be sent back to London?'

'Of course not. You've got school, and Fern, and there are lots of other plans for the summer.'

'You wouldn't lie to me, would you?' she asked with a trace of her old anxiety.

'Have I ever?'

Gemma considered her reply. 'No,' she eventually admitted.

'There you are, then. Off you go back upstairs, and no more talk about running away.'

'I won't,' Gemma promised, 'and I hope you find your file soon.'

Louise picked up Gemma's discarded backpack. She peered inside. She had packed a pair of pyjamas, a small amount of money in her purse, and her iPlayer. Louise sank back into her chair, her legs no longer able to support her. She didn't dare imagine what could have happened had Gemma managed to run away. She sat up straight as realisation kicked in. She didn't care if Charlie was in another of his moods — Gemma's welfare was more important than his volatile temperament. She dialled the restaurant extension.

'Have you seen the news?' Charlie said before she had a chance to speak.

'What? No.'

'Harry was full of it. I suggest you turn on the television.'

15

Louise stared in disbelief at the images flickering across the screen in front of her.

'Celebrity chef Charlie Irons, ignominiously dismissed from his cookery slot on daytime television, has suffered a further blow, this time to his personal life,' the news announcer was saying. 'His grandfather, the man he revered for having first promoted his interest in cookery, has been outed as a thief and a fugitive from the law. Reports received from an anonymous source reveal that Grandpa Irons was not the hardworking figure Charlie had created, but a common criminal.'

The kitchen door crashed open, as a furious-faced Charlie filled the doorway. 'Is this your doing?' he demanded.

Louise was forced to raise her voice to match his. 'Of course it isn't.'

'Then where did they get this information?'

'I have absolutely no idea.'

'Don't answer that,' Charlie ordered as the telephone began to ring. He was breathing so heavily it was making him red in the face, and Louise began to fear he might suffer a seizure.

Fern poked her head round the door. 'Louise, it's a lady called Saffron Weekes for you. She sounds like Mrs Young when she's cross with us.'

'Give me that.' Charlie snatched the receiver out of his daughter's hands before Louise could move.

Fern widened her green-blue eyes in shocked surprise. 'What's wrong with Daddy?' she hissed as he strode past her and into the hall, closing the connecting door behind him.

'He's upset about the restaurant.'

'Is it true what they're saying about Grandpa Irons?' she continued to whisper, as if fearing she would be overheard. 'Gemma and I have been watching television in our bedroom. Was he really a criminal?' Fern asked in an awed voice.

Louise evaded a direct answer. 'Shouldn't you be getting on with your project?'

'Gemma was going to get some leaves for me, but you stopped her going out, so I'm stuck.' She crossed her arms and planted her feet firmly on the floor in an open gesture of confrontation.

Charlie came back into the kitchen. 'Fern, upstairs.'

'But Daddy, I want to — '

'I said upstairs, and turn the television off.'

With another startled look at her father, the child scuttled away.

'What did Saffron have to say?' Louise asked, dreading the answer.

'Much the same as I did. She wants to know what's going on.'

'I don't know.'

'According to her, you've stolen her research and sold it to the highest bidder.'

'That's not true.'

'Isn't it?'

'It wasn't like that — and if you don't

211

believe me, where's the file now?'

'I don't know. You tell me.'

'I've been looking for it for days. Someone must have removed it from my office.'

'You expect me to believe that?' Charlie curled his lip in scorn.

'It's the truth. That's why I was so worried when the key disappeared.'

'You mean this one?' He snatched up the key Gemma had left on the table and thrust it under Louise's nose.

'Yes,' Louise replied in a hoarse voice.

'Can you explain what it's doing here if it's supposed to be missing?'

There was no way Louise could provide an explanation unless she implicated Gemma. After a long pause Louise admitted, 'I can't.'

'I hope you were paid a fortune for your exclusive.' Charlie's voice was bitter. 'Because it's going to have to last you a long time. Your career is finished.'

Louise made one final attempt to convince Charlie she was innocent.

'You can think what you like about me, but I didn't sell your story to anyone.'

The telephone began to ring again. Louise didn't dare make a move to answer it.

'That thing stays unplugged.' Charlie yanked the lead out of the wall in one vicious movement.

'Mummy wants to talk to you, Daddy,' Fern trilled from the doorway, looking reluctant to enter the kitchen.

'I'll take it in the restaurant.' There was a cold draught as, without a look in Louise's direction, Charlie slammed the kitchen door behind him.

Fern now tiptoed into the kitchen. 'Is Daddy very cross with you?'

'A little.' Louise did her best to smile but it didn't work well.

'Did you sell Grandpa Irons's story for lots of money?'

'No, of course I didn't.'

Millie flicked her tail against the bare flesh of Louise's legs and mewed plaintively. Louise bent down and tickled her behind her ear. The cat began to purr, and nudged her head into Louise's hand.

'Now you know what it's like when no one believes you,' Gemma said; she was standing on the threshold with a smile of triumph on her face. 'It's not nice, is it?'

'At least Louise didn't tell on you about the office key,' Fern turned on her, 'and she could have done. That's why Daddy didn't believe her story about the file. He thought she'd lied about the key. If you don't go and tell him you stole it, I will.'

'I *didn't* steal it.' A look of panic crossed Gemma's face.

'Yes you did.'

'I've never been in the office.'

'You're lying again.'

'I'm not.'

Louise clenched her fists. 'Go back to your room please, girls, and get on with your homework.' She kept her voice as steady as she could.

'Will you tell Daddy about the key, Louise?' Fern did not look in the mood to give up without a fight.

'If the opportunity presents itself. Now off you go, the pair of you. I'll come up and see you later.'

'I'm not helping you with your wretched project,' Gemma grumbled to Fern as they climbed the stairs. 'I hate the countryside.'

'If you don't like it, you can always go back to London,' Fern snapped back. 'No one wants you here.'

Louise heard a bedroom door slam and then silence. Charlie's voice behind her made her jump.

'That was Pia on the line. Did she tell you we were getting back together again?'

'She did mention it,' Louise admitted.

'Is this what this is all about? Are you getting your own back because you thought I had used you?'

Louise was finding it difficult to follow Charlie's train of thought. 'No.'

'Because if you did, you've been wasting your time.'

'Charlie, please, I don't understand

what you're talking about.'

'Pia invented the story about our great reconciliation.'

'Why?'

'Her jealousy was one of the reasons our marriage failed.'

'Why should she be jealous of me?'

'She suspected I might be falling in love with you.'

Louise's cheeks flamed. 'That's ridiculous.'

'I agree.'

Louise felt as though she had been stabbed in the chest by Charlie's words.

'So you see, you didn't have to go to the lengths you did to blacken my grandfather's name.'

Unable to speak, Louise turned away from him. Everything seemed very quiet outside. She wondered if the workmen had heard their raised voices. The windows were open and the sound of their argument would have carried across the courtyard.

'Pia also mentioned,' Charlie continued, 'that she's decided not to attend our opening night — if there is one.'

Louise could feel their world falling down around them and it was all her fault. 'We could try issuing a denial,' she suggested.

'Every word of the story is true,' Charlie admitted in a voice Louise barely recognised.

'What?'

'The trauma my grandfather suffered as a child left him with a lifelong fear of authority. Is it any wonder he ran away to the other end of the world when he was accused of being a thief by the powerful father of the girl he wanted to marry?'

'But don't you see that doesn't make him a common criminal?'

'He was totally innocent, but for many years he was too scared to come back to clear his name. And you know the old saying about there being no smoke without fire? People will start to wonder how he managed to set up a flourishing business and bring up a young family. Where did the money come from? They don't want to know that he worked eighteen hours a day to give me a good home, a better start in life than he had. That sort of detail is inconvenient, and certain sections of the press have never let facts stand in the way of a good story.'

'Charlie, I'm so sorry,' was all Louise could think of to say.

'I'm going out.' He grabbed his leather jacket off the hook.

Louise had no idea how long she stood by the open back door after the roar of Charlie's car engine died away.

* * *

'Louise,' a voice whispered against her ear.

'Wassat?' She dragged herself out of a deep sleep. It took her several seconds to realise she was lying fully clothed on her bed and shivering with cold.

'Are you awake?' the insistent voice demanded.

'What time is it?' she croaked,

218

groping for her alarm clock.

'Half past five. Did you know you've got all your clothes on?'

'Fern?'

'You're wearing your shoes. You're not supposed to do that. You'll tear the bedspread. It was ever so expensive. Mummy will be cross.'

Fern was wearing her nightdress and hopping from one foot to the other. 'My feet are cold.'

'What are you doing out of bed?' Louise asked.

'I didn't want to tell Daddy because he's been so grouchy.'

'Tell him what?'

'It's Gemma. She's gone.'

16

Louise was instantly alert. 'Gone where?'

'I said some horrid things to her, Louise.' Fern's lip wobbled. 'I didn't mean them, but I was so upset when you got the blame for things you didn't do, and then she wasn't very nice about you. We had a huge argument, and I went to sleep in my old room 'cause I didn't want to sleep with her. Then when I woke up, I crept back to our shared room to say I was sorry and could we be friends again, and she wasn't there.'

Louise scrambled off the bed. 'Perhaps she went to sleep on the sofa downstairs.'

'She's left a note.' It was then Louise noticed Fern was clutching an envelope. 'It's addressed to you.'

Louise snatched it out of Fern's

finger and, switching on the bedside light, scanned the contents.

'What does it say?'

'I have to talk to your father.'

'He's not in his room either,' confessed Fern. 'His door's open and the bed's empty.'

'Do you have any idea where he is?' Louise wasn't sure she could think clearly in the face of so many shocks.

'I think I saw a light across the courtyard.'

'Fern,' Louise said as she shrugged on a jacket, 'go back to bed.'

'I'm not staying in the house alone. I'm coming with you.'

'Then get dressed quickly. We have to find Gemma.'

Fern scampered off, leaving Louise to reread Gemma's letter.

'I'm going away,' she had written. 'I didn't steal the office key. I found it in the kitchen under the biscuit tin and I kept it. I know I shouldn't have. I'm sorry you got the blame for the missing file as well. I didn't take it. I know you

221

don't believe me because I stole those things from the shops. Don't try and find me. I'm not coming back. Ever.'

Louise dreaded to think how long Gemma had been gone.

'I'm ready.' Fern had shrugged on some leggings, a warm jumper and a woolly hat.

'Come on then, let's go.' Louise snatched up a torch, and they ran across the forecourt in the direction of a light that was shining through one of the upper restaurant windows.

'I think that's Daddy's shadow on the wall.' Fern banged on the door. 'Daddy, it's me,' she called out.

'Fern?'

'We have to talk to you. It's important.'

Louise trained her torch on the window. 'Charlie,' she said as she restrained Fern, 'we can't find Gemma.'

The restaurant window was flung open with such force it went crashing back against the brick wall. Charlie poked his head out and put a hand to his eyes to protect them against the strength of the flashlight. 'What's going on?' he said.

'We think Gemma snuck out after we'd all gone to bed,' Louise explained. 'She left a note saying she's sorry for all the trouble she's caused. Charlie, she's run away.'

'It was Gemma who took the office key, Daddy.' Fern wriggled free of Louise's grasp. 'That's why Louise couldn't tell you. She's not a sneak.'

'When did you last see Gemma?' To Louise's relief, Charlie didn't waste time asking inane questions.

'I looked in on the girls at about ten,' Louise volunteered.

'We had a big argument, Daddy,' Fern confessed, 'so I went to sleep in my old room.'

'Do you think she'll try to make her way back to London?' Louise asked, dreading to think of any consequences.

'Stay there. I'm coming down.'

'Perhaps we should ring Pia's parents,' Louise suggested as Charlie yanked open the restaurant door. From the dark circles under his eyes and the stubble on his chin, she guessed he hadn't been to bed either.

'What was all that about a letter?'

Louise passed it over. 'Her writing's wobbly and smudged. I think she might have been crying.'

Charlie crunched it up and dropped it on the ground. 'I'll do a search of the outhouses.'

'I'm going to ring Alice Tolley,' Louise said.

'Why?'

'I don't know, but it's better than doing nothing.'

'Go on, then. Fern, come with me. We'll start with the stables.'

Alice answered the telephone on the second ring. 'No, dear, I haven't seen her. Would you like Arthur to take a look round? We're both early risers so you didn't wake us. Arthur, get the car out. Don't argue; we've got an emergency on our hands. It's young Gemma.'

Charlie and Fern were back before

Louise had replaced the receiver. 'No luck,' he said.

'Alice hasn't seen her either. She and Arthur are going drive round in the car and see if they can spot her. Charlie, we're going to have to call the police.'

'She can't have got far. Fern, are you absolutely sure you've no idea where she could've gone?'

'You don't think . . . ' Louise began slowly, scared to voice her fears.

'What?' Charlie demanded as she faltered.

'She was friendly with some biker boys.'

'For heaven's sake, talk sense. She's a child.'

'She's not a child. She's a growing teenage girl.'

'And I suppose you know all about teenage girls.'

Charlie's words stung Louise into retorting, 'I was one once, so I know a little more about them than you do.'

'Louise stopped Gemma running away before — twice. I think it might've been three times, actually. That's why Gemma was cross with her. It's probably why she took the key too.' Fern's voice tailed off as Charlie stared at her, aghast.

'Is there anything else going on that I should know about?' he asked in a stone-cold voice.

'She only pretended she was part of the biker gang because she didn't have any real friends at school, so I don't think she's run away with them,' Fern said. 'I was the only one who spoke to her. I think she's been ever so unhappy.'

Louise felt sick in the pit of her stomach. Why had none of them realised how desperately lonely Gemma had been?

'She likes your uncle Rocko,' Fern volunteered. 'He's kind to her.'

'Rocko's good to everybody.' Louise poured boiling water over the pot of tea she had been making.

'I'm going to have another look outside,' Charlie said.

'I can hear the telephone.' Fern leapt

to her feet. She looked at the blank space on the wall. 'It's gone.'

Louise glanced to where Charlie had thrown the handset onto the top of the fridge. Fern sniggered.

'That was Daddy, wasn't it? He does get cross sometimes.' In the background the telephone continued ringing. 'I'll answer the one in the hall. I bet it's Gemma calling.'

Louise sagged against the kitchen sink and stared out of the window. The forecast was for a sunny day. She shivered, wondering if she would ever feel warm again.

'It's Mrs Young,' Fern's voice was full of awe as she handed over the receiver. 'And she wants to speak to you.'

'Mrs Young,' Louise spoke hurriedly down the line, 'I'm going to have to call you back. We need to keep the line free.'

'Don't hang up,' Mrs Young spoke equally as quickly. 'I have Gemma.'

'What?'

'Yay!' Fern began to dance a jig.

'Where?'

'The caretaker was doing his rounds and spotted one of the windows was open. He discovered Gemma in my office and called me.'

'Thank goodness.'

'I'm going to text Daddy.' Fern began hunting round for Louise's mobile phone.

'Are you still there?' Mrs Young asked.

'Yes, sorry.'

'She's been going through my things I'm afraid, but she won't speak to me. I think she might have been looking for money, but we don't keep any in the school overnight.'

'I'll be right over.'

'No need. Mr and Mrs Tolley have just arrived, and with your permission they're happy to drive her back.'

'Thank you, Mrs Young. Is Gemma okay?'

'Apart from not speaking to anyone, she seems fine. By the way,' Mrs Young added, 'I posted your envelope. Shall I give your file back to Mrs Tolley? It was caught up with Fern's project.'

'What envelope?'

'I found it together with a file full of private papers. It was mixed up with Fern's latest coursework. Of course I didn't read the contents, but the envelope was stamped and ready to go.'

'Can you remember to whom it was addressed?'

'I'm sorry, I can't.' Mrs Young sounded uncertain. 'I hope I did the right thing.'

'We can talk about it later,' Louise reassured the anxious headmistress. 'And thank you for everything. I hope this doesn't mean Gemma will be unwelcome at the school again.'

'I don't like to feel I've failed any child, and Gemma is a bright girl and shows lots of promise. She'll settle, given time. You know she thinks the world of you.'

'I beg your pardon?'

'She talks about you a lot when she's in the mood. Anyway, I'm sure she'll be fine after some breakfast and a good sleep. There's Mrs Tolley now.' Mrs Young cut the call.

'Anyone home?'

'Rocko!' Fern squealed.

'We were passing by after an all-nighter and we thought we'd deliver our reply to your invitation personally. Is that tea on the go?'

'Hello, darling.' Nancy swept Fern up in her arms and gave her a kiss. 'My, you get up early in the country, don't you? Have you got lots of exciting plans for the day?'

'It's Gemma,' Fern said in an excited voice. 'She's run away.'

'Has she?' Nancy raised her eyebrows.

'Mrs Young found her. That's our head teacher.'

'Hey, that's cool.' Rocko smiled. 'I can't count the number of times I played truant, 'cept I did it the other way round. I ran away from school.'

'This is serious, Rocko,' Louise said, then kissed Nancy on the cheek.

'Just trying to lighten the mood. I've been hearing things aren't so good up here at the moment. The invitation thing was an excuse. I've come to offer moral support.'

'Why don't Fern and I go watch some television,' Nancy suggested, 'and leave you guys to talk?'

'It's been terrible, Rocko,' Louise confessed as Nancy closed the door behind her.

'Storm in a teacup.' Rocko opened the biscuit tin and peered inside.

'It's more than that.'

'I suppose you got the blame for whatever went wrong?'

'Charlie thinks I sold the story of his grandfather's past to the press.'

'Right, let me get at him.' Rocko banged the biscuit tin down on the table. 'He needs to be put right on one or two things.'

'No, Rocko.'

'I'm not standing by to let him have a go at my girl.'

'I didn't do it, Rocko.'

'You don't have to tell me that.'

'It seems the papers got mixed up with Fern's school project. I don't know what happened, but the headmistress found an envelope and posted it. She can't remember to whom it was addressed, but I think that's how the media got hold of the story of Charlie's grandfather.'

Charlie stumbled through the door. 'Fern says Gemma's been found. How did you get in?' He glared at Rocko, who glared back.

'I understand you've been accusing Louise of being a thief.'

'Mrs Young's found Gemma,' Louise butted in, fearing the situation could turn nasty. 'Alice and Arthur are driving her home now. And it was Mrs Young who posted Saffron's envelope to the press.'

'There.' Rocko was all smiles again. 'My lovely Louise is as innocent as the day she was born. Now does the Drew family get an official apology from you, Mr Irons, or am I going to have to write a protest song about you and sing it to the nation?'

Laughter floated through from the lounge, where Nancy and Fern were watching television. Charlie poured out a mug of tea and sat down. 'My grandfather was innocent too,' he said after a pause.

'Is that an apology?' Rocko said.

'He fell foul of his employer when he started courting his daughter. I think he was fitted up. Money went missing, and the finger of suspicion was pointed at my grandfather. His flight would have been taken as an admission of guilt.'

'No sense in going over old ground, I always say.' Rocko smiled at them both. 'And I'm glad we're all friends again.' He finished his biscuit. 'Time I should be going. I've got to tell you, Nancy's been practising a couple of new numbers for your celebrations, and the boys are raring to go.'

Charlie blinked at Rocko as he stood up and broke into a broad smile. 'Here comes the lovely Alice.' He opened his arms and embraced her before she had a chance to recover herself. 'I hear you've been on a rescue mission. Hi, Arthur,' he called over her shoulder, 'and Gemma. Got a hug for old Rocko?'

Gemma ran to him and locked her arms around his waist.

'Everything's fine,' he said as he patted her head. 'We're all here and we all love you, so no running away again. Promise?'

Gemma mumbled a response into his shirt. Rocko eased her hold on his waist.

'We didn't hear that, but no matter.'

'Gemma!' A human catapult tore across the room as Fern launched herself at the girl.

Nancy strolled into the kitchen after her. 'Hey, the gang's all here. Isn't that great? We'd better get going, Rocks. It's getting a mite crowded.'

'We must be leaving too,' Alice Tolley said. 'By the way,' she added, delving into her bag, 'here's your file, Louise. Mrs Young says she's sorry she kept it, but after she posted the envelope it completely slipped her mind. Come along, Arthur. See you later, Rocko.'

'It's a date, Alice.'

Louise felt a cold hand slip into hers. She squeezed Gemma's fingers.

'Sorry,' Gemma whispered. 'Are we still friends?'

'Only if you promise never to run away again.'

'I won't.'

Louise stroked Gemma's cheek and smiled into her tired face. 'Good, because I'd be lost without you.'

'You would?'

'You and me against the world?'

'You're on.'

Charlie clapped his hands. 'Right, I'd like a bit of attention here please.'

Fern groaned audibly. Louise cast her a stern look. 'You two girls need a warm bath,' she said. 'I'll put the water on.'

'Correction,' Charlie interrupted Louise. 'Fern, I'm putting you in charge of baths; and Gemma, you are to do exactly as my daughter says.'

'But I'm older than her,' Gemma protested.

'What are you going to do, Daddy?' Fern asked.

'Louise and I need to talk.'

'Come on, Gemma.' Fern grabbed her elbow. 'They're going to have another argument.'

'Then I'm staying,' Gemma said with a mutinous glare at Charlie.

'Look, I promise to play things by the rules,' he said. 'Now will you please leave us?'

Gemma stood her ground. 'Give me a good reason.'

'Don't you know anything?' Fern gave all the appearance of a woman of the world as she explained, 'Daddy might want to kiss Louise again after he's said he's sorry and all that.'

Gemma turned bright red, and Louise could feel her complexion colouring up too. She didn't dare look at Charlie.

'Mummy gave me some lovely bath bubbles for my birthday. I'll let you share them, but only if you come now.'

Fern tugged a reluctant Gemma out of the kitchen, leaving Louise and Charlie to face each other alone.

17

Louise, her face flaming, began to sidle towards the door. 'Perhaps I ought to keep an eye on the girls.'

Charlie blocked her path. 'I'd rather like to get what I have to say out of the way now.'

'I need a shower.'

'I wouldn't argue with that statement, but the girls will probably pinch all the hot water.'

Louise stood indecisively between the table and the door. 'Look, Charlie,' she said in a firm voice, 'I'll save you the trouble of getting everything off your chest.' She knew it was important to choose her words carefully. 'It was my responsibility to look after the girls, and I failed miserably, especially with Gemma.'

'We all let Gemma down,' Charlie was quick to point out, 'so don't beat yourself up about that.'

'If anything had happened to her . . . ' a sob caught in her chest. Charlie made a movement towards her, but Louise warded him off. 'Let me finish.'

'Go on, then.'

'I shouldn't have misplaced the key to the office or lost Saffron's file. How it came to be mixed up with Fern's project, I'm afraid I don't know.'

'At one time or another almost everything's landed up on the kitchen table. I'm surprised more hasn't gone astray.'

'But my carelessness caused Gemma to run away. Can't you imagine how that makes me feel?'

'I've a pretty good idea,' Charlie agreed, 'because I feel much the same way about myself. We can't change the past. The best thing we can do is to make sure it doesn't happen again — and together we can do it.'

'No, we can't.'

'Why not?'

Louise tucked a strand of hair behind her ear. Charlie didn't seem to be getting the message. 'It was my carelessness that caused your grandfather's past to become public knowledge.'

'So?'

'Your credibility's been thrown into disrepute.'

'We're getting into the realms of big words, and I told you I'm not very good at them.'

'I'm serious, Charlie.'

'So am I.'

'Then don't you realise what this means?'

'One thing all this bad-mouthing of my grandfather didn't reveal was his forgiving nature. He wouldn't have cared two hoots about all this upset, and he certainly wouldn't have blamed you. It took Gemma's disappearance for me to feel the same way, and to realise what really matters in life.'

Louise wished Charlie's eyes weren't so deep blue and that they didn't have the power to make her lose concentration. 'Was your grandfather the reason you were so publicity shy?'

'It was partly that, and coupled with my marriage to Pia, I grew wary of the press.'

A silence fell between them. Louise tried to ignore the buzzing sensation in her ears. How much longer would she be welcome at Brooks Farm?

'Where do you think Pia got the idea we were an item?' Charlie asked after a few moments.

'I don't know.' Louise didn't think it was possible to feel so confused.

'I do.'

'Do you mind if I open the back door?' Louise asked. 'I need some fresh air.'

'Morning, Louise.' The foreman gave her a cheerful wave. 'I hear from Alice and Arthur that you've had quite a night.'

Louise did her best to return his smile.

'Glad Gemma's back safe and sound. Teenagers.' He rolled his eyes. 'I've a couple of girls myself, so I know what a trial they can be. Still, it'll be worth it when one day you wake up and find you've got a very pleasant young woman on your hands.'

Louise cast a furtive glance at Charlie, but his eyes were fixed firmly on the table.

'Best get on,' the foreman said.

Charlie now looked up. 'I'm not quite ready to join you,' he called out.

'I'll make a start on your checklist then, shall I?'

'Fine. I'll catch up with you later.'

Louise's face was still uncomfortably warm after the foreman had gone off to change into his boiler suit. 'I think I'd like to sit down,' she said, pulling out a chair.

Charlie nodded. 'Where were we?'

'You were saying you'd like me to leave as soon as possible.'

'I don't remember saying anything of the sort,' Charlie objected.

'You were about to get round to it.'

'As a matter of fact, I was about to say that Pia was absolutely right.'

'About what?'

241

'She's nobody's fool when it comes to these sorts of things.'

'What sort of things?'

'Pia stirred things up with her story about us getting back together because she wanted you out of the way. I know it's not logical, but that's the way she thinks.'

'Why?'

'Why did she want you out of the way?' Charlie asked. Louise nodded. 'Because she realised this time my feelings were serious. Fern's noticed it too. She takes after her mother at times,' Charlie added with a suggestion of a smile.

Outside, Louise could hear more workmen arriving. Their cheerful chatter floated through the open window. Millie nudged open the back door and, spying Louise, headed towards her. Swirling her tail in the air, she investigated some milk that had dripped off the table and onto the floor and began to lap it up.

Louise forced her attention from Millie back to Charlie. 'Would you mind repeating that?'

'I can do better than that. Why don't you stand up?'

'What for?'

'Because I'd rather like to kiss you. Actions speak louder than words, and I can't do it when we're both sitting at a breakfast table surrounded by mugs of cold tea, pools of milk and a thirsty cat.'

'No.' Louise shook her head.

'No what?'

The legs of her chair scraped the floor as she pushed it backwards. It fell over with a crash.

'Now you'll have to stand up, unless you want to wind up in an undignified heap on the floor,' Charlie said.

'I need to do something,' she said, unable to come up with an excuse to leave the room.

'No you don't.' Charlie stood up slowly and pushed his chair neatly under the table. 'That's the way to do it. Now why don't you come round my side of the table?'

'I can't.'

'Then I'll come round your side. Get

out of the way, Millie.' The cat gave an indignant meow as he nudged her fur with his leg. 'There,' he said, moving in closer. 'That wasn't too difficult a manoeuvre, was it?'

'You have to stop now.'

'Why?'

'It's not . . . ' She searched for the right word. ' . . . appropriate.'

'It never is, and I can't wait for an appropriate moment forever, so why don't I do what I said I'd do, then we can discuss issues later?'

Before Louise could move, Charlie's lips descended on hers. She felt the stiffness leave her tired limbs as the heat from his body warmed her aching heart. It was something she had wanted Charlie to do for a long time, which didn't make any sense at all. They were polar opposites. No way should she be attracted to him, nor him to her. And hadn't he said the whole idea of him falling in love with her was ridiculous?

A loud clang followed by a muffled oath in the yard outside drew Louise out of her dream and back into the reality of the moment. 'We mustn't do this.' She dragged herself out of his embrace.

'Yes we must.' Charlie was forced to raise his voice above the noise level outside.

'I can't believe your arrogance.'

'Now what have I done?'

'You seem to think I'm prepared to fall into your arms because it's been proved that I didn't steal Saffron's wretched file and I didn't sell on details of your grandfather's past to the media. From the moment I arrived here you've accused me of all sorts of things. You can hardly expect me to feel grateful now everything's been resolved to your satisfaction.'

'That's a lot to expect of anyone, I agree. I think I was trying to give myself reasons not to like you. Silly, I know, but that's the only explanation I can come up with.'

'You haven't even apologised — for anything.'

'I thought I had, but I'll do it again if you like. I really am sorry, Louise, for all the accusations I made against you. Will that do?'

'Stop it,' Louise implored.

'I've had another idea. I'll post an apology on social media, and with a bit of luck it might go viral.'

'You don't do social media.'

'I'll get the girls to help me. Louise?' Charlie wasn't teasing her anymore. 'We've got something good going here. Don't sacrifice it for the sake of your pride.'

'My pride?' Louise felt ready to explode.

'Sorry to interrupt,' the foreman said as he poked his head through the open door. 'Only, we have a minor crisis out here.'

'Deal with it,' Charlie snapped.

'Think it's an A and E job — badly crushed toes; and as your car's in the forecourt, Charlie, could you do the honours? Or if you're busy, perhaps Louise could help out? It is a nasty injury and does need to be seen to,' he prompted when neither of them moved.

Muttering under his breath, Charlie grabbed his keys. 'On my way,' he called over his shoulder, then turned back to Louise. 'You needn't think we're finished here.'

The foreman made a discreet exit.

'No running back to your parents, or Rocko, or anywhere else. I'll only come after you, so it'd be a complete waste of your time.'

Fern burst into the kitchen a few moments later, followed by Gemma. 'Where's Daddy gone?'

With her head still reeling, Louise stared at the girls in bewilderment. 'There's been a minor emergency,' she explained.

'We're hungry,' Fern said, dismissing Louise's explanation as if it were of no importance.

'I could make us bacon sandwiches,' Gemma offered with a shy smile at Louise. 'It's the only thing I can cook.'

Pulling her wits together, it was all

Louise could do not to cry out in relief. She had temporarily lost sight of the bigger picture. Gemma was home. She was safe. That was all that mattered. The girl was dressed in a pink top and leggings. Her freshly shampooed hair was shining with health, and without the sulky look on her face she looked like a normal teenager.

'I'm hungry enough to eat two bacon sandwiches,' Louise admitted. 'But first I have to freshen up.'

'You do look something like Millie dragged in.' Fern giggled. 'I'm surprised Daddy wanted to kiss you.'

'Fern,' Gemma said, glaring at her, 'you weren't supposed to say anything.'

'Sorry.' The girl put a guilty hand to her mouth. 'We were crouching on the stairs. At first we thought you and Daddy were having one of your arguments, so we stayed put. Then when he started kissing you, we didn't think it would be nice to break things up.' Fern began to snigger. 'Was it nice?'

'Get the bacon out of the fridge,'

Gemma ordered, 'and don't ask silly questions.'

'I only wanted to know,' Fern protested.

'And I'll need some bread.'

'Stop being so bossy.' Fern dragged her feet towards the bread bin. 'I think I preferred it when you were horrid.'

Unable to resist hugging Gemma, but feeling it might be a step too far, Louise gave her shoulders a squeeze. 'It's lovely to have you back, darling,' she said. 'And I haven't forgotten my promise about our day in town.'

'Just the two of us?' Gemma asked.

'What about me?' Fern protested. 'I don't see why I should be left out.'

'How about we arrange another date and you can choose what you'd like to do?' Louise held her breath, hoping Fern wasn't going to make a fuss.

Fern put some bread down on the table. 'There's a place in the arcade that does face painting. A girl in my class had hers done in all sorts of different colours. Mrs Young was cross and made her wipe it off, but if I had it done at the weekend it wouldn't matter, would it?' She inspected the contents of the fridge. 'Where's the bacon?' she called out.

'Was it all my fault?' Gemma asked Louise, the fearful look back on her face. 'The trouble between you and Charlie?'

'Nothing was your fault, Gemma,' Louise reassured her.

'I caused a lot of problems, didn't I?'

'Yes, you did,' Louise acknowledged, refusing to downsize the extent of Gemma's actions. 'But it's all over now, so we won't mention it again. And I want your promise that if you have anything on your mind, you'll come to me. There's nothing we can't talk through together.'

'That means you're staying then, doesn't it?' Gemma was smiling again.

'Of course she's staying. Daddy wants her to,' Fern said as if that were an end to the matter.

Louise realised she had made a

tactical error and that the girls had backed her neatly into a corner. 'I'll be down in five minutes, so get those sandwiches on the go.' Leaving the girls squabbling in the kitchen, she went up to her room, sank onto her bed, and wearily pulled off her blouse.

Common sense told her she should walk away from Charlie Irons and Brooks Farm, but in her heart of hearts she knew she didn't want to. Charlie had admitted he was falling in love with her, and she knew she had been in love with him since she couldn't remember when.

Going into the bathroom, she switched the controls on the shower to hot. Then after standing under the steamy water for a few moments, she flicked the temperature to cold, hoping the spray would revive her jaded senses. The pungent aroma of eucalyptus filled the shower cabinet as she massaged shampoo through her hair. Then, stepping out of the shower, she towelled herself dry.

With her hair neatly styled and

wearing her smartest black trousers and white top, she felt ready to face the new day — whatever it would bring.

18

The bacon sandwich Louise was clutching slipped from her fingers and fell to the floor.

'Was that your breakfast?' A pale-faced Saffron Weekes greeted her with a smile as she stopped pacing backwards and forwards. 'Sorry, I didn't mean to startle you.' She eyed Louise's mug. 'Coffee? Mind if I have a sip? I've been on the go for hours.' She sniffed appreciatively. 'This is the real thing too, isn't it? Best Brazilian?'

Louise threw what was left of her bacon sandwich into the bin. A quick glance at the wall clock told her it was only half past nine. How could so much have happened in such a short space of time?

'You're wondering what I'm doing in your office, aren't you?'

'The thought had crossed my mind,'

Louise admitted.

'I sneaked in. I hoped no one would be on site. Silly, I know. I mean, half nine in the morning?' Saffron made a face. 'Get real.'

'Your point is?' Louise nudged the woman, who had lapsed into silence.

'I was going to write you a note, but now you're here . . . ' Saffron took a deep breath. ' . . . can we let bygones be bygones?'

'Did I hear you correctly?' Louise stuttered.

'I hope so. I'm offering you an abject apology.'

'Just like that?'

'I don't know of any other way. I know we have bridges to build, but I'm trying to take the first step, if you'll help me.'

'In case you'd forgotten the details, let me remind you of a few facts.'

Saffron grimaced but said nothing.

'You had an envelope sealed, stamped and ready to go in that file you gave me. When it was inadvertently posted, you blamed me for the fallout when all along you knew what had happened. You also knew that if the contents of the envelope went public, they could bring about Charlie's downfall.'

'I know, and I accept full responsibility for the consequences.' There was none of the superficial media professional about Saffron now. 'At first I really did think you'd read the contents of the envelope and decided,' Saffron floundered, 'to make your mark.'

'By shopping Charlie?'

'I was angry. I should never have accused you.'

'No, you shouldn't have. You were the guilty party. You were the one who was going to go public, weren't you?'

'It was at the back of my mind, but I don't think I would've seen it through. I truly am sorry for all the trouble I've caused, and I'd like to put what happened behind us.'

'You should be apologising to Charlie, not me.'

'I would if he was here.'

'So if you made your fortune on your exclusive, what are you doing hanging about apologising? Shouldn't you be sunning yourself on a private beach somewhere in the Caribbean?'

'You make it sound so sordid.'

'How else would you describe what happened?'

'If you must know, I wasn't paid a penny. The report was anonymous.'

'You'll have to forgive me for being short on sympathy.'

'I suppose I deserve nothing less,' Saffron replied, lowering her eyes.

'Well now you've had your say, don't let me keep you.'

'There's something else.'

'Yes?'

'Our sponsors have hit a cash crisis.' Saffron's words came out in a rush.

'Did these sponsors send you here today to maximise the damage limitation?'

'No. I'm here on my own agenda.'

'I see.'

'I've messed up, haven't I?'

Louise acknowledged her words with a faint shrug.

'The envelope wasn't supposed to be in the file I gave you. I panicked when I realised what had happened. Then when I was called into the director's office, I feared the worst, but the sponsors had other things on their minds. They've withdrawn their funding.'

'You mean no more Sub-Plots?'

'That's right.'

'And you're out of a job?'

Saffron nodded, her eyes suspiciously bright.

Louise's antagonism softened. 'I'm sorry.'

'That's incredibly generous of you.' Saffron looked as surprised as Louise felt.

'I know what it's like when no one wants to know you,' she replied. 'And it must've taken a lot of courage to come here today.'

'I nearly didn't make it,' Saffron admitted.

'What are you going to do now?'

'I'm putting out feelers like mad. If you need any media research, I'm your person.'

'I'll bear your offer in mind.' She saw no further point in bearing a grudge against her old adversary. Deep down she admired her for accepting responsibility for what had occurred.

'Good luck with the restaurant,' Saffron said. 'Or should I make that break a leg?'

'If I do, you'll have to take my place.'

'My pleasure.'

'Here.' Louise scribbled her name on an invitation card and passed it over.

'What's this?'

'The dress rehearsal party is tomorrow night, if you can make it.'

'Really? You're on.' Saffron now looked like an excited child.

'There'll be lots of people here, but not many in your field of work I'm afraid.'

'Right now I'm not in the mood for media types. Thanks for the invite.' Saffron waved it in the air. 'See you at the party. *Ciao.*'

With her head still in a spin, Louise did her best to immerse herself in the last of the tedious admin. Resolutely refusing to think about Charlie's early-morning declarations or the turn of events with Saffron, she set about the task of finalising the latest figures onto the spread-sheet.

'We're off now,' the foreman called up to the open window, his voice alerting Louise to the time.

She waved back at the gang of departing workmen. Without the constant blare of radios and the whine of power tools, the courtyard fell eerily quiet. And with no outside influences to distract her, Louise's thoughts drifted back to the earlier scene in the kitchen.

What had Charlie been thinking of, kissing her? And with Gemma and Fern crouching on the stairs listening to every word? She wriggled with embarrassment at the memory and wished she hadn't enjoyed the experience quite so much.

'I'm back.' As if by magic Charlie appeared in the doorway. 'And glad to find someone is still on site. It's like the *Marie Celeste* out there.'

'The workmen have gone,' Louise explained in a business-like voice, hoping Charlie wasn't considering taking up where he left off.

'So I can see.' In contrast to Louise, he seemed perfectly composed as he sauntered in to the office.

'How did you get on at the hospital?'

'One very sore foot, but the good news is we're not about to be sued for negligence. It was a nasty accident, but no lasting damage done.'

Louise fiddled with some paperwork on her desk, uncertain what to say next.

'Why don't you stop pretending you're busy?' Charlie suggested.

'I'm not pretending. There's a lot to do.'

'No, there isn't. Everyone else has sloped off. I'm the boss, and what I say goes. And I say the shop is closed for the day. Now, do you have something glamorous to wear for the big night?'

'I'm sure I'll find something suitable in my wardrobe.'

'Something suitable isn't good enough.' Charlie shook his head. 'What I'm looking for is glamour with a capital G. So as I've given you the afternoon off, I suggest we hit the shops.'

'We can't take off without a word to anyone.'

'Fern and Gemma and Alice Tolley have gone in search of leaves for the next stage of Fern's project. Personally I think they've got the wrong season, but I wasn't about to discourage them. They've packed up a picnic lunch and won't be back for hours. That only leaves Millie, and I'm sure she can manage without us. So are you ready? To ease your conscience, a fresh batch of promotional leaflets has arrived, so we'll hand them out as we go round.'

'Charlie, there's something I have to tell you.'

'What?'

'We've had a visit from Saffron Weekes.'

'What did she want?'

'To apologise, and to tell us that Sub-Plots has folded.' She held up a hand to stop him from interrupting. 'I think I said all that needed to be said.'

'Then why are you still looking worried?'

'Were Sub-Plots going to help out with financial backing?' Louise voiced the question that had been nagging at the back of her mind ever since Saffron had told her the financiers had pulled out.

'It was never an option I took seriously,' Charlie reassured her. 'You remember that day I visit the bank?' Louise nodded. 'The good news is we're not over-extended. In fact the manager's promised to bring his wife to the opening-night party.'

'If there is one.'

'I'll admit Pia's got cold feet, but it was touch and go whether or not she was going to come anyway. You haven't received any other cancellations, have you?'

'No, but supposing no one turns up on the night?'

'Then we'll throw another party and invite Alice's granddaughter and her entire school over to eat everything up. Does that satisfy you? Now was there anything else?'

'I've invited Saffron to the dress rehearsal party.' Louise flinched, ready for an explosion. 'And she's promised to come.'

'Good for her.' Charlie grinned. 'If you'll turn the computer off — ' He gestured towards Louise's screen. ' — we'll be on our way.'

★ ★ ★

'Where do we start?' Louise asked after they parked the car in the multi-storey.

'With these, I suppose.' Charlie thrust a bundle of flyers at her.

'Excuse me,' a young mother pushing a baby buggy said as she approached. 'You're Charlie Irons, aren't you?'

'What can I do for you?' Charlie

replied, smiling at her and the youngster.

'I loved your cookery slot. My mother and her friends did too.'

'How very kind of you to say so.'

'That Louise Drew wasn't a patch on you. Do you know she couldn't even set jelly?'

'You don't say,' Charlie drawled.

Louise swiftly disappeared behind a convenient pillar, her ears burning, and not daring to emerge in case the young mother recognised her.

'Why don't you bring your mother and all your friends down to my new restaurant, the Dover Soul?' Charlie suggested with a smile. 'We're opening next week.'

'I think it'd be a bit out of my price range.'

'With one of these leaflets, you can get a special deal. We're doing a children's menu as well, and there'll be lots of other attractions. There's even a competition, and the prize is a complimentary dinner for two.'

'Can I bring my partner?'

'Bring the whole family.'

Charlie's fan trundled off, happily clutching a handful of extra leaflets that she promised to distribute at the school gate.

'Did you hear what she said about me?' Louise said when the young mother was safely out of earshot.

'You never told me you couldn't set jelly.'

'It was strawberry, and it slipped out of my hands onto a white carpet. I think that's when the producers decided I had to go.'

Another group of excited females accosted him. 'Charlie!'

Louise stepped back, not wanting anyone else to recognise her, and watched as he signed autographs and posed for selfies.

'Here, we'd better put these on,' he said after they finally departed eagerly reading Charlie's leaflets and promising to visit his restaurant as soon as they could. 'It's not much of a disguise, I know, but it may just work.' He produced two baseball caps. 'Pull yours down over your eyes and maybe we won't get recognised.'

An hour later they were through.

'I don't think my feet will ever speak to me again.' Louise perched on a convenient bench and rubbed her sore toes.

Despite their precautions, Charlie had been unable to prevent the more eagle-eyed shoppers from recognising him, and their progress had been halted several times.

'At least now we can get down to the serious business of the day: dresses. No time to rest up.' Charlie dragged Louise to her feet. 'What do you think of this one?' He paused by the window of a discreet boutique.

'We can't go in there,' Louise protested.

'It's a shop, isn't it?'

An assistant glided forward, smiling at Charlie. 'Yes, sir. Can I help you?'

'The dress in the window?'

'The model?' the assistant corrected him. 'A model denotes individuality,' she explained.

'Is that so?' Charlie's face lit up. 'Well, Ms Drew would like to try on your model please.'

'Of course.' The assistant raised her hand, and a junior member of staff immediately removed the model from the window and disappeared behind a curtain.

'Will the model be featuring in the publicity shots of your new restaurant, Mr Irons?' The assistant allowed herself a brief smile, indicating a leaflet someone had left by the till.

'As my personal assistant, Ms Drew will be hosting the evening,' he replied with the faintest suggestion of a wink at Louise. 'And of course she'll be in all the photos.'

'Then I'm sure we can come to a suitable arrangement,' the assistant almost purred her reply. 'If Ms Drew would care to come this way?'

* * *

Their shopping finished, Louise and Charlie were seated in a small coffee shop tucked down a side street. At their feet were several bags, the largest containing the blue-and-white cocktail dress that had fitted like a dream. Charlie had insisted on buying the matching shoes to go with it.

'I cannot believe you did that,' Louise said with a chuckle.

'Did what?' Charlie sampled a biscuit. 'This is good — soft and buttery, with a tang of lemon I think.'

'Structured a deal with the boutique.'

'It's sound business practice. They'll get free publicity, we get a model for you to wear, you have your photo taken, and we credit the boutique. Winners all round. Hey, this coffee's good too.' He replaced his cup in the saucer. 'Now, about us.' He leaned forward, his piercing blue eyes fixed on her.

Louise felt a lump lodge in her throat and swiftly swallowed some coffee to ease the blockage.

'It's time we took up where we left off this morning.'

'Not here.'

'We've done the angst. We've had the row, the misunderstandings, and all the other nonsense.'

'Do you know the girls were listening on the stairs when we were talking?'

'You mean when I was kissing you?' Charlie did not look in the least abashed.

'They seem to think . . . ' Louise looked around as if seeking inspiration.

'What?'

'That I'll be staying on permanently.'

'Good. I'm glad that's settled.'

'But it isn't.' Louise hadn't meant to raise her voice. She blushed as several of the customers cast inquisitive glances in their direction.

'If you're worried about Pia, I have to tell you she's going to be based in Italy for the foreseeable future, so she shouldn't be too much of an interference regarding our domestic life.'

'But she's Fern's mother and Gemma's aunt.'

'Agreed, but she always looks for the easy option.'

'I'm not sure I like being referred to as an easy option.'

'Then how about being referred to as my wife?'

Louise cast another anxious glance around the coffee shop. 'People are looking at us.'

'Let them.' Charlie took a deep breath. 'I know you like things cut and dried, so I'm going for it now. Louise Drew, will you marry me?'

19

'I don't know what I'm eating.' Rocko's cheeks were bulging and he had a huge smile on his face. 'But it tastes much better than cold baked beans.'

'It's a salmon roulade. Want to try another? We've got mini-fish and chips if you fancy something more substantial.' Louise waved the canapés under his nose.

'Why don't you leave the plate with me?' Rocko eyed the nibbles greedily. 'Guitar playing is hungry work.'

They were standing on a makeshift stage positioned in a corner of the courtyard. The evening sun was beating down on them, and beads of perspiration glistened on Rocko's brow. The band had taken five while he performed his solo.

'Have you got enough water?' Louise asked.

'We have a dispenser full of the stuff.' Rocko leaned towards her and asked in a conspiratorial whisper, 'Who's the guy in the fancy bow tie chatting up Nancy?'

Louise widened her eyes in horror as she looked in the direction of Rocko's pointed finger. 'What's he doing here?'

'If he's a gatecrasher, you only have to say the word. I don't like the way he's got his arm around Nancy's waist. Want me to take a pop at him?'

Louise put out a quick hand to restrain Rocko. 'He's a food critic, but his invite was for the opening night, not the dress rehearsal.'

'Important, is he?'

'He could make or break us, and we've already upset him once.'

'In that case, let's give him another night to remember.'

'Rocko, don't do anything sensational.' Louise tried to detain him, but it was useless. She recognised the signs. Rocko was on a roll.

'What's the dude's name?'

'Quentin Voisin.'

'Right.' Rocko grabbed the microphone. 'Quentin Voisin to the stage, please. Quentin Voisin.'

'No,' groaned Louise, her face in her hands as people began to look round to see what the disturbance was about.

Charlie was instantly by Louise's side. 'What's going on?'

'You don't want to see this,' Louise mumbled.

'My party — I make the rules.'

'It's Rocko.'

'What's he done now?'

'He's inviting Quentin Voisin on stage to play the drums.'

'Then you were wrong, Louise. This I have got to see.'

'He's not supposed to be here, and you said we weren't to upset him.'

'I don't remember that.' Charlie whipped off his chef's whites and tossed his toque onto a checked tablecloth.

Louise had another go at distracting him. 'Shouldn't you be panicking in the kitchen?'

'I thought I'd have a tantrum out

here instead.' His smile stretched from ear to ear. 'But it looks as though I've been outclassed by Rocko. This is going to be a blast.'

'That's what I was afraid of.' She groaned again as Rocko picked up his treasured guitar and strummed a chord.

'It's cabaret time!' He punched a salute. 'Are we ready?'

A happy roar greeted his announcement.

'Today we have an extra-special guest, our very own Quentin Voisin on drums. Give him a huge Brooks Farm welcome, folks.'

Beaming behind his tortoiseshell glasses, Quentin twirled a pair of drumsticks in the air and executed one of the neatest drum rolls Louise had ever heard. 'I don't believe it,' she gasped as Rocko swung into his routine.

'It looks like old Quentin can actually play,' Charlie agreed.

'Those are my drumsticks,' Louise protested. 'Rocko's got no right to hand them out to a perfect stranger.'

'Nothing you can do about it right now. Come on, if I can chill out so can you.'

Louise opened her mouth to protest, then gave in. 'Quentin does seem to be enjoying himself.'

'Then why don't we follow his example, leave everyone to it, and go somewhere quiet?'

'We can't abandon our guests.'

'They seem to have abandoned us,' Charlie commented. A surge of bodies flattened them against a barn wall as everyone pushed forward to get a better view of the stage. 'I do hope opening night is a little more dignified.'

'If Rocko's running the show, then you've got no chance.'

'I was afraid you'd say something like that.' Charlie glanced towards the stage as another roar went up. Nancy, resplendent in rhinestones and wearing the tightest dress Louise had ever seen in her life, sashayed to the centre of the stage and, after blowing kisses at everyone, picked up the microphone.

'Is everyone having a good time?'

A cheer drowned out the rest of Nancy's speech.

'Okay, folks,' she finally made herself heard, 'this one's for two of the nicest people I know, Charlie Irons and Rocko's niece, the lovely Louise. They're over there hiding by the barn. Let's hear it for them.'

All eyes swivelled in their direction.

'It's to Charlie we owe this wonderful evening. And my good friend Quentin here — ' She blew the bespectacled critic an extra kiss. ' — had better give the Dover Soul a five-star review. If he doesn't, we have video evidence of tonight's excesses. You have been warned, Quentin.' She wagged a stern finger at the blushing critic.

'She really is something else, isn't she?' Charlie said as he looked on in admiration.

'We all love Nancy.' Louise returned her cheerful wave.

'One more thing, folks,' Nancy began.

'Hurry up, darling,' Rocko bellowed. 'My strings are getting impatient.'

'You'll like this one, Rocks.' Nancy extended her arms wide. 'My two young friends here — ' She indicated an excited Fern standing beside an equally excited Gemma. ' — inform me that Charlie and Louise have an important announcement to make this evening.'

Louise turned to Charlie, a horrified look on her face. 'Did you put the girls up to this?'

'No, this is your fault,' he said.

'How can it be my fault?'

'When I proposed marriage, you promised me an answer tonight.'

'Not in front of everyone! And how did Fern and Gemma find out?'

'I told them.'

'You had no right to do that.'

'And Gemma told Nancy.'

'Why did she do that?'

'Because like everyone else round here, she wants you to stay on. And Gemma had the idea that if we got married, it would seal the deal. So what's it to be?'

'Come on, everyone's getting a mite impatient up here,' Nancy's voice crackled over the microphone. 'And unless you want a riot on your hands, LuLu, I suggest you give Charlie an answer — and it had better be the right one.'

'I think with Nancy and the girls on my side, I'm onto a winner, don't you?' Charlie smiled down at Louise.

'Charlie Irons, you are looking unbelievably smug,' she retaliated.

'Louise,' he said, his voice softly urgent, 'you can't keep me in suspense any longer. Will you marry me?'

'I've almost a mind to say no.'

'But you won't, will you?'

Louise was glad the barn door was supporting her back. She sagged against Charlie's shoulder. 'Ask me again.'

'For the third and last time — Louise, will you marry me?'

'I will,' she said in a soft voice.

'Guess what?' Charlie murmured against Louise's ear. 'I've got the key to the office in my pocket.'

'Why?'

'Well you could say I didn't want it going astray again, but actually I'd rather like to kiss you, and that's something I don't fancy doing in front of an audience.'

'But what about your guests, the party, the food?'

'It's all taken care of.' He waved towards Nancy.

'Do we have a result?' she asked.

'It's yes,' Charlie called.

'Clever girl, Louise — right answer.' Nancy blew her another kiss. 'Now, business of the day over . . . ' She turned back to the guests. ' . . . it's time to party.'

Seizing his opportunity, Charlie grabbed Louise's hand. 'Ready?'

'But . . . ' Louise began.

'Come on,' Charlie insisted, 'otherwise I'm going back on my promise.'

'What promise?'

'Not to kiss you in front of everybody. So what's to be?'

279

As if in reply, Quentin performed a drum roll. Nancy swung into her number, and Rocko went into his routine.

Louise raised her eyebrows. 'This way?' She gestured.

'You're on.'

Charlie grabbed her hand and, ducking down to avoid being seen, they crept past the buffet and towards the office.

We do hope that you have enjoyed reading this large print book.

Did you know that all of our titles are available for purchase?

We publish a wide range of high quality large print books including:
Romances, Mysteries, Classics
General Fiction
Non Fiction and Westerns

Special interest titles available in large print are:
The Little Oxford Dictionary
Music Book, Song Book
Hymn Book, Service Book

Also available from us courtesy of Oxford University Press:
Young Readers' Dictionary
(large print edition)
Young Readers' Thesaurus
(large print edition)

For further information or a free brochure, please contact us at:
Ulverscroft Large Print Books Ltd.,
The Green, Bradgate Road, Anstey,
Leicester, LE7 7FU, England.
Tel: (00 44) **0116 236 4325**
Fax: (00 44) **0116 234 0205**

Other titles in the
Linford Romance Library:

WISHES CAN COME TRUE

Angela Britnell

Meg Harper is shocked when the man she knows as Lucca Raffaele, who stood her up in Italy the previous summer, arrives to stay at her family home in Tennessee — this time calling himself her step-cousin, Jago Merryn ... Jago is there to acquire a local barbecue business, but discovering the woman who came close to winning his heart is only one of the surprises in store for him. Can they move past their mistrust and seize a second chance for their wishes to come true?